profile

kelly cheek

Cover and book design by Kelly Cheek

ISBN: 978-1-7335022-0-7

Fiery Muse Publishing
Littleton, Colorado 80129

Printed in the United States of America

Acknowledgments

I'd like to take full credit for this novel. But even though mine is the only name appearing on the cover, it wouldn't have been possible without the help, guidance and encouragement of others.

First and foremost, I'm thankful for the unseen presence of my muse throughout the creative process. The idea for *Profile* appeared almost fully formed, and poured out with greater ease than anything I've ever written.

As I trolled Facebook under my alter ego, purely for research purposes, there were several people who unwittingly helped me by not reporting me and getting me kicked off of Facebook.

To all of you, thank you.

Facebook estimates that between 4.3% and 7.9% of its monthly active users were individuals signing in with more than one account. It has been suggested that between 5.5% and 11.2% of all accounts on Facebook are either duplicate, malicious, or otherwise 'fake.'

Based on Facebook's own figures, this means that anywhere from 67 up to 137 million monthly users are not as they may seem at first.

Do you know who you are talking to when you log in every time?

L ate autumn in Denver was a grab bag. We could have a sunny day in the 60s, and the next day could be freezing or snow. Today was just grey and cold. The Monday morning sun was distant, yet it still made a feeble attempt to push its rays in at a slant through the tinted glass of the conference room. But the meager sunlight was enough to make the mahogany table warm to the touch.

I didn't really need that, though. I was already feeling kind of warm.

But in a good way.

"Mike is moving on to, well, I won't say greener pastures," Ed Leeson, my boss, was saying at our Monday morning staff meeting. "Argosy Advertising is pretty lush and green," and he smiled at his cleverness, "but Mike's moving to *different* pastures anyway." Okay, so that wasn't the part that made me feel warm. That just made me squirm in embarrassment for Ed.

Mike Jellison gave the requisite grin toward the boss, acknowledging his wit. Mike was the senior art director at Argosy, a scrawny man a head-and-a-half taller than me. For the last couple of years, Mike had fawned over Ed, laughing at his jokes, complimenting his vast intelligence. If Ed wore a jeweled ring, Mike would probably kiss it daily. I'm surprised Mike's nose didn't have a permanent tan, and I don't mean from trips to Mexico.

"We wish him the best of luck and success in his future endeavors. But that means that in two weeks, there will be an opening here at Argosy that will have to be plugged," Ed continued. "And we won't be hiring an outsider for the job. So the position is going to be filled by either Arden or Joe."

That's the part that made me warm. Not Joe. I mean Joe Polaski is okay. We got along alright, even worked on a few projects together. He's a regular guy you could joke around with or be serious with. And he had the intelligence to understand the difference and give the proper response. Sometimes. We'd even gone out for a beer after work on a few occasions.

I guess you could say we were sort of friends.

Too bad, in a way, because now, we were up for the same job. That's right, in case you hadn't guessed by now, I'm Arden. Arden Chase. A cool name, I know. I assure you, though, I don't really live up to it. I mean I try to be cool, but the nerdy artist persona has kind of haunted me since high school. And that was thirty years ago.

Anyway, Ed was still going on and on about picking the right man for the job, giving our best for the company, and all that canned corporate bullshit. But I admit that after hearing that I was up for Senior Art Director, I kind of tuned him out.

My job used to be okay. I used to be one of the 'creatives,' doing design and illustration for various high-profile accounts. A few were even seen nationally. On a shelf in my office, there were four Addies, and I was primarily responsible for two of the Clios in the glass cabinet in our lobby. Not bad for our little agency.

All of those awards had provided leverage for getting me a few raises and a promotion to junior art director, and I now took home some pretty good money. But I also now hated my job. I hadn't won any awards in a while. As one of the junior art directors at Argosy, I had some veto power, and I offered a certain amount of direction to the creatives. But I wasn't a creative myself any longer. Not really.

That's the way if felt to me anyway.

Oh, sure, some argued that art directors are creative, and I agree that we are creative in some ways, in deciding on the style of a project, for instance, the direction it should take. Determining how to do a job.

Hence the term 'art director.'

But it's just not the same as back when I was a designer/illustrator, when I was actually doing the work. Drawing the lines, applying the color. Making those directions come to life.

Now, I felt like I was more administrative than creative. A desk jockey. Pencil pusher.

I don't know, maybe it's just me.

But at Argosy Advertising Agency, or 'Triple A' as some of the clever admins called it, or 'A Cubed' as a couple of the *really* major geeks referred to it, the Senior Art Director, besides overseeing the juniors, was also given his choice of design jobs, and was allowed the necessary time out from his 'administrative' duties to actually execute them. Kind of a perk for the position.

And the pay was even better.

I don't know what more Ed said after that. Like I said, I tuned him out. But the next thing I realized, the meeting was over.

"Good luck, asshole," Joe Polaski said with a crooked grin as we filed out of the conference room. Yeah, he was kind of jerk, but we got along fine.

"Thanks, Joe," I said. "You too."

Once we were out of the conference room, we all went our separate ways. I walked down the hallway that was, as of this morning, lined with tinsel and plastic holly. Felicia, the receptionist, had been busy putting up Christmas decorations while the meeting was going on, and now the whole place gleamed with tinsel.

And plastic.

My office came up on the left. I knew it was *my* office because my name was on the door. "Arden Chase – Art Director."

Whatever.

The sprig of plastic holly that Felicia had taped over my door was already coming loose and hanging crooked into the doorway. I pushed the holly back up and burnished the tape down with my thumbnail. I went inside and closed the door.

I usually kept it closed, but people still came in. The door, unfortunately, didn't have a lock.

It was an okay office – not huge but roomy and well-appointed. Along one wall was a series of shelves that showed off a number of projects for which I had won accolades – and awards. And there in the middle of it all were the four American Advertising Awards I had won. The stylized star-shaped "A" on each of the Addies looked a little dull and tarnished now. It had been a while. I was in a slump.

Yes, that slump has lasted three years now. So what?

I was ready for a change.

As I looked at the pile of sketches and comps on my desk, work that had been done by the creatives and was awaiting my approval, I sighed as I leaned forward to start going through them.

Really ready for a change!

* * *

The drive home was usually a long one. Northbound I-25 was always a slow drive this time of day. I lived in Boulder, proudly described locally as 'twenty-five square miles surrounded by reality.' It was a popular destination for hippies in the sixties, and that free-spirit mentality has been a part of Boulder culture ever since then. Situated right at the foothills of the Rocky Mountains, it's the site of various athletic events and music festivals, as well as such refined affairs as the Polar Bear Plunge and the Naked Pumpkin Run.

Boulder was only about thirty miles from downtown Denver, but it usually took me at least an hour to drive.

Gave me plenty of time to wonder what I would be walking into when I got home.

It was likely that Evelyn would be unhappy about something. My wife was just an exceedingly unhappy person.

Usually, she was unhappy about me.

Nowadays, it seemed like we fought all the time. Oh, not in the traditional sense of the word 'fighting.' It was always more one-sided than that. I usually remained pretty quiet in an effort to not provoke her, but it seemed as if I usually provoked her by remaining too quiet.

"You don't ask about my day," she might complain. "You don't ask how I'm feeling. You don't give a shit about me!"

Having been through this countless times before, I would not respond immediately. Instead, I would try to foresee how she might react to any possible response I could make. But then, my delay in responding would be taken by Evelyn as a confirmation of her accusations, which only made her angrier.

In time, I had finally learned to try to be cheerful when I came home, ask about her day, and so on. Yeah, it took a while. I'm not very bright. But something would still trigger a reaction.

I mean, it's not like we fought every day. But thinking back at the end of a week, I could usually count on one hand the days that we *didn't* have a fight or the post-fight freeze out. With fingers left over.

One time last week, I almost lost it. Evelyn was yelling at me about something I said about her herbal supplements. Evelyn is a stressed out person, and she bore a particular disdain for medical doctors. Instead, she made regular visits to a chiropractor, a massage therapist, and an acupuncturist. She also took herbal supplements to the tune of almost 70 pills a day. Yes, I counted them. All told, she spent over a thousand dollars every month on her herbal supplements and natural practitioners.

Now I don't have a problem with somebody going the natural route. Hell, I've tried a couple of natural remedies and actually noticed benefits myself. But over a thousand dollars every month, to treat a generally healthy person? It seemed a little over the top to me.

But I made the mistake of saying something about it.

She railed at me for over an hour about that, and as she did, I tried to tune her out. Where I almost lost it was that I found myself recalling an old Bill Cosby routine I had seen on TV, where he was talking about his wife having a 'conniption.' He then proceeded to give a comical description of her face splitting apart as she grew even angrier at him, and I almost smiled at the memory.

Fortunately, I caught myself before I gave in to the smile. I knew the danger of Evelyn's reaction if she saw me smiling while her whole world was falling apart, so I forced the Cosby routine from my mind.

My marriage to Evelyn Parsons was initially fueled by the heat of a physical attraction that seemed to start fading within just a couple of weeks. The first signs of her depression appeared and I found that I was incapable of doing anything right in her eyes. The first time I suggested that she get professional help – well, let's just say that was one lesson I learned quickly.

After our first few fights, I admit I almost left her, and that was before the marriage was even a month old. But then we got the news that Evelyn was pregnant, a result of the heat of our initial passion.

Lanelle was born a couple of months before our first anniversary, a sweet and cheerful addition to our family. She became the target of Evelyn's affection, and while I missed being the recipient of it as I had been at the beginning, I did appreciate the discontinuance of our almost nightly ritual of fighting. Lanelle became the focus of our mutual love, and in sharing that common interest, we found some happiness together.

I realize that sounds kind of cold and detached. I don't want to give the impression that I considered Lanelle to be just a shock absorber, a bulwark against Evelyn's unhappiness with me. The fact is I love my daughter very much. But as far as Evelyn and I were concerned, Lanelle was the only thing holding us together.

When Lanelle reached about two years of age, she became independent and rebellious. I'd heard the term 'terrible twos,' and Lanelle embodied it very well. As a stay-at-home mom, Evelyn was the primary one who had to deal with it, and I found that, once again, I became the target of her anger and the cause of her unhappiness. I knew I could be an idiot at times, but even I was surprised at how little I could do right.

So it was actually a relief when we found that Evelyn was pregnant again.

Even back then, we didn't have sex very often, so it was a pretty simple matter to pinpoint when it happened. We had actually talked about having another child, a sibling for Lanelle, and on that one night, we managed to not fight, at least long enough to get the job done. I don't know if it was the hormones or just the knowledge of her pregnancy, but Evelyn actually became tolerable again.

Then came the miscarriage.

After Evelyn lost the baby, followed by the news that she could no longer have children, well, that's when things kind of went down the toilet for us again. I can't say I blame her. I know the ordeal was particularly hard on her, and I really did try to be understanding and help her through it. I *can* be a real sweetheart.

But either I was also an incredible moron, or there was just no helping her. Or she didn't *want* to be helped.

She *seemed* like she did. For a while, Evelyn became quite a reader. She read books like *Codependent No More*, *Women Who Love Too Much*, and various other books I can barely remember. But nothing changed. Nothing except that Evelyn, armed with a little popular psychobabble, now thought she was an expert on behavior and the workings of the human mind. Which gave her more ammunition to use against me.

Now, I don't want you to think that our entire time together was bad. I do have good memories with Evelyn, even beyond the initial honeymoon period. But those times had gotten to be very few and far between.

Oh sure, I had often thought about leaving Evelyn, but I loved Lanelle and decided to stay for her. I found plenty of ways to put up with Evelyn's frequent bouts of displeasure, many of them involving work. In fact, as it turned out, my need for time away from Evelyn coincided perfectly with my promotion to junior art director at Argosy.

Of course, the fact that I was spending more time at my job meant that Evelyn now had to deal with Lanelle by herself for longer periods of time, which got on her nerves, and which in turn made for more fights when I *was* home. That was no fun. But at least I gradually learned not to strike back.

Our arguments became more one-sided, with Evelyn venting her indignation upon me and me quietly taking it like a man. Despite the old adage about not adding fuel to the fire, this sometimes made Evelyn even angrier, which I have to admit gave me a little bit of sadistic satisfaction.

But at least our fights did seem to burn out a little quicker.

One improvement was that, with Lanelle sleeping a couple of rooms away, Evelyn usually kept the volume down.

Another improvement had nothing to do with Evelyn, or Lanelle. That was when Cyndi Shelton, a young divorcee, moved in next door. God, she was hot! And I don't know if it was my own male ego or what, but she seemed attracted to me too. After a few brief conversations across the picket fence dividing our yards, I often found myself fantasizing about her.

Especially after one particular encounter.

It was in the early summer, and Cyndi was out working in her flower garden while I was doing some other yard work. I can't even remember for certain what I had been doing. All I could remember was the outfit she was wearing.

Her back was almost completely bare due to the little halter top she wore. Then there were the shorts that showed her perfect, shapely brown legs, and that rode up in back when she bent over her garden.

Her auburn hair gleamed like fire in the sunlight, and she had an enchanting way of flipping it back over her shoulder when it got in her way. Some kind of sinuous motion that I loved to watch.

I made sure that I was facing her direction as I pulled weeds or trimmed hedges, or whatever the hell I was doing.

Even now, I can remember imagining the feel of my hands on her back, and on the perfect curve of her ass, which I could glimpse just a little bit of when she bent over. I felt a heat, a stirring, a shortness of breath that I remembered but hadn't experienced in several years with Evelyn.

Cyndi almost caught me looking. I had been wearing sunglasses, so I was able to cover it up pretty easily, but when she came to the fence to visit, I was again glad for the dark glasses.

Her midriff was slightly damp and glistening, her beautifully sculpted abs shimmering from perspiration in the early summer warmth. Her eyes were a wondrous golden-brown color, and they crinkled a little on the sides when she smiled, which she did a lot.

I admit I was smitten.

Then a cool breeze from the mountains brushed across her and her nipples suddenly pressed hard and prominent against the fabric of her halter top. I'm pretty sure my erection had sprung up just as quickly. I can't be certain if her smile was a response to that, or to some brilliantly witty remark I had just made.

Or maybe it was just my imagination.

One thing I can be sure of, though, is that the memory of those early encounters with Cyndi could always be counted on to return whenever Evelyn was raking me over the coals about something.

Lanelle left for college in California a few months ago, and without her presence as a buffer, it felt as if Evelyn was coming down even harder on me. At times, when I felt like I could safely offer recommendations, I suggested that she try to find a hobby, something to focus her time and attention on.

Anything to get her mind off of how fucking awful her life was.

But it was fairly useless. Evelyn had never had any real interests, few friends and very little creativity. With Lanelle gone now, Evelyn had too much time on her hands, and little with which to fill it.

* * *

Shit, I don't know where all that reflection came from, but it helped to pass the time anyway. Because I was now approaching my house. That's it there, the stone and stucco Mid-Century Modern house near the crest of the hill, set back from the street with the long curving, aspen-lined driveway, and the picture windows that looked out on a view of the Flatirons.

Pretty nice, huh?

Evelyn just had to have it. She came from a fairly well to do family. Her father had been a lawyer, and she was accustomed to having nice things.

A few years back, when we first bought the place, I couldn't afford the down payment, so her parents had helped us out. I was hesitant at first, didn't want to be beholden to them. But Evelyn was insistent. Her old man kind of drove a hard bargain, too. The mortgage was higher than I had ever been accustomed to. I didn't know how we could keep up with the payments, and we had to make a few cuts. I gotta tell you, that made for some stress early on.

But it all worked out.

That's not to say that I didn't like the house. It was a great place, in a nice, upscale neighborhood. There was a certain glow of pride that I always felt whenever I told someone where I lived.

That place had set us back a bit, but I guess it was worth it. I mean yeah, it's a nice house with a killer view, but there was also a nice den. A room of my own where I could retreat, and Evelyn, well she almost never followed me in there.

As I approached, I cast a glance at Cyndi's house. But it was December. The flowers were long gone. She wasn't out.

Damn.

I pulled up my driveway and into my garage, ready to engage.

* * *

Well, I'm happy to report that the evening was one of the uneventful ones. That's not to say it was pleasant. Evelyn was still mad at me about our fight last night. I had had the audacity to suggest we have sex. It had been over a year.

Really.

She was still a somewhat attractive woman, although she had put on a few pounds, as she often lamented. Her blondish hair looked kind of disheveled at the moment, but for the purpose of sex, that just seemed appropriate. She was across the room from me reading a magazine when I broached the subject.

"What do you think about conjugating tonight?" I asked. I never said I was romantic.

Without moving her head, she looked up at me with a 'you must be joking' expression.

"I can't make love to someone I don't respect," she had responded with a disgusted sigh, then looked back down at her magazine. She really had a way of making me feel good about myself.

"That's fine," I replied. "I never said anything about making love. How about we just have sex?"

After my ill-considered suggestion, she railed at me for a couple of hours. Then we went to our respective beds, sans sex.

Dinner tonight was very quiet and cold. But at least my evening didn't get derailed by another fight, or by a continuation of the previous one. I made a quick statement that I had work to do, to which Evelyn made no reply at all, not even a grunt of acknowledgment. I didn't care. I was quickly installed in my den.

Starting up my laptop computer, I logged into Facebook to see what was going on. I had lots of friends on Facebook and I could often spend at least an hour, usually more, just looking at the things people posted. Some were political, and I may or may not agree with them. Some were off-color, and usually funny. Some were just plain dumb.

"Getting ready to leave for work now."

So the hell what?

Folks who took the time to post inane messages like that, or details about what they were eating for dinner, or the cryptic messages like, "I'M SO MAD!!!!!" but with no other details, just begging people to indulge them and ask what's wrong, well I just didn't have time for those. I always scrolled through those very quickly.

There were a few people who I followed fairly closely, though, so that I was notified of their posts and could go check them out first thing. One was my brother, Benson, down in Colorado Springs. (Benson Chase. Yeah, he had a cool name too.) Some were people that I had gotten to know on Facebook and liked. Some were just really clever and posted things that I liked reading or looking at.

Then, there was that little message icon, indicating that I had a personal message waiting for me. Clicking on it, I saw that it was from Chaisang.

I don't remember when she had become a Facebook friend. But she had sent me a message about a week ago and we started chatting. She lived in Thailand and was thirty years old, almost twenty years younger than me.

And she was really pretty.

I know what you're thinking. And it wasn't like that. Our chats had always been very tame. Nothing sexual or suggestive. Nothing off-color in the least. We just got to know each other, what we liked to do, the kind of food we ate. Things like that. It seemed like a nice bit of stability in my miserable life.

Chaisang seemed to like me, and she often let me know that she was happy to have me as her good friend.

"Hi hello to my good friend Arden," she wrote. "How are you today?"

I knew it was fourteen hours later there. I looked at the clock. It was almost nine o'clock, so it was mid-morning tomorrow in Thailand. A quick glance at the column on the right and I saw that she was currently online.

"Hi Chaisang," I replied. "I'm fine. How are you?"

"I fine, but little sad."

She did that fairly often, and as you probably guessed from what I said about those cryptic, uninformative messages just a few minutes ago, it kind of got on my nerves. But she was cute so I tolerated it.

"Why are you sad?" I asked.

"My sister mean to me. She say not get me gift for my birthday."

This was the way a lot of her messages had been lately, hoping for a present for her upcoming birthday. With her limited grasp of English, I couldn't be certain if her comments were in a materialistic vein and she was hinting that I send her a present (how was I going to manage that?), or if she was just relating what's on her mind.

Lately, I had started ignoring those parts of her messages.

"I'm sorry," I typed. "How is your day going?"

There was a long pause, which seemed to be fairly common when I didn't continue on her train of thought. While I was waiting for her response, I got another message, from somebody else. Jolene Danzig. I remembered when I received her friend request just a couple of days ago. Another very pretty girl, about twenty years old.

There was very little information on her profile page, and only two pictures, but the girl was gorgeous. The picture she used as her cover photo, the banner that ran across the top of the page, was of her in a negligee, lying face down on her bed, propped up on her elbows, a coy little smile on her lips. In the other photo, her profile picture, it looked as if she was naked, sitting on a sofa, clutching a large pillow in front of her. All the sensitive parts were covered, yet the picture was definitely titillating.

I had approved the friend request right away, then didn't see anything from her for a while. Curious, I clicked on the message to read it.

"hello"

"Hi, Jolene," I responded. "Nice to meet you. Where do you live?" As I said, her profile page contained almost no information.

"i live america. where you live?"

I was a little baffled by that, because my profile page contains all kinds of information about me, probably more than it should. I was also suspicious because of the sentence structure. Didn't seem like that sentence was written by an American.

"I live in America, too. In Boulder, Colorado."

"i usually live with my dad, but i now staying with gramma in Romania."

Huh.

"looking for good man."

Okay, first of all, before we get to this statement, let me just say that people who don't bother to use correct capitalization and punctuation irritate me. It demonstrates a lazy, lackadaisical attitude, and disrespect for the English language, and for their readers. But at the same time, I realize that a lot of people chat on their phones, and capitalization can be bothersome. *I* still do it, but I can overlook it.

But 'looking for good man'? My profile clearly stated that I'm married. It also clearly showed my photographs, including a couple of me with Evelyn. I mean, I don't think I look bad for forty-nine years old. In fact, I've been told several times that I look at least five years younger than that.

But this girl is easily less than half my age. What could she possibly see in an old codger like me? And she's gorgeous. She could probably have any young man she wanted. So I was suspicious.

And I was flattered.

"Well," I typed, "I wish you success in that. But I'm married."

"so"

This was getting kind of weird, but I was curious to see where it went.

"So, if I took up with you, I wouldn't be a very good man anymore."

"why?"

"People tend to look down on men who cheat on their wives."

"you still with you wife?"

"Yes. I mean I'm alone right now, but yes, my wife and I are still together."

"bible say man have many wives."

What the hell does the Bible have to do with this?

"Well, first of all, Jolene," I replied, "that was a long, long time ago. And secondly, that's not really allowed in the United States. And I'm pretty sure I wouldn't be able to convince my wife to go for it."

That mention of Evelyn had almost the effect of a bucket of ice water in the crotch. Even though our marriage was a miserable sham, I had never cheated on her. In time, we had gradually settled into a dull routine. A sort of 'friends with benefits' relationship, if you considered occasional episodes of soul-searing hatred a benefit.

Okay, I didn't.

But I quickly recovered the feeling of intrigue when I saw Jolene's next message.

"you don't love me?"

Okay, this chick was definitely a little loopy. But I remembered her photos and decided to play along.

"I don't even know you. How can I love you yet?"

"you want me go?"

"No, I didn't say that." I pulled up her photo again, the one where she's naked behind the pillow. "But we don't know each other. If anything, after seeing your pictures, I lust for you, and I'm definitely curious about what's behind the pillow in your profile picture."

I felt a weird feeling of excitement as I typed that, a slight shortness of breath, and I was surprised. I hadn't felt that flutter in a long time.

"What can you tell me or show me that would make me feel differently?" I continued.

"you have cam?"

"A web cam? Yes, I do."

"yahoo?"

I wasn't sure what she meant by that.

"You mean the web browser?"

"the chat"

The chat. I didn't know any more than I did before.

I did a quick search on my computer and didn't turn up anything like Yahoo Chat. I opened a new browser window and searched online, and the first thing that came up in the search results was "Yahoo Messenger." Quickly reading the description of the program, I decided it sounded like what she might be referring to. I clicked on the link and started downloading and installing it right away.

"I found a Yahoo Messenger," I typed. "Is that what you mean?"

I looked back at the progress bar. It seemed to be a quick installation. It was almost finished already.

"open it" Jolene typed.

She was really taking charge, now.

I opened it and the program performed an initial setup. I created a user name, and within a minute or two, I was connected with Jolene. And there she was, on the same sofa that was in her profile picture. She also had the pillow in front of her, but I noticed she wasn't naked behind it. Not completely, anyway. I could see bra straps. I turned the volume down low. Didn't want Evelyn hearing this.

"Hi, Arden."

"Hi, Jolene," I said.

I could feel the shortness of breath again, when I thought about what I was doing here. I mean, I wasn't *really* being unfaithful to Evelyn. I didn't think I was trying to justify it. It was the truth! I was just talking to a pretty girl.

Who happened to be nearly naked.

Then I felt almost defensive. So what if I'm doing this! Evelyn's practically brought it on herself. Refusing to have sex with me for over a year? What does she expect? I am a man, after all. I have needs too!

Before I could give any further thought to it, Jolene moved the pillow a little so she could position her computer a little better.

Oh god! That sweet young body in just her underwear!

"You like what you see?"

"Yes, Jolene, I like it very much!"

"Want see more? Show me you."

26

Okay, I realized then that I hadn't really thought very far ahead.

In a flash, I thought about my situation, and I listened for any sound outside my den. Evelyn often went to bed pretty early, depending on her state of mind. I've heard that depression can manifest itself in different ways with different people. One of the ways was in the form of fatigue, and that's the way it often did with Evelyn. The house was completely quiet. I decided that she must have gone to bed.

I looked back at the video image on my computer monitor. Jolene had hooked a thumb under one of her bra straps and was toying with it, teasing me. She was looking at me slyly, out the side of her eyes, with a little smile. She pulled the strap down a little, exposing the top of her breast, then moved it back up.

I took a deep breath to calm my nerves, and started unbuttoning my shirt. Jolene smiled as I opened it up and showed her my chest.

"Nice," she said.

Yeah, I worked out a little.

"Is more?"

I hesitated for a moment, my breaths coming a little heavier, and just for encouragement, Jolene pulled the strap down. Seeing her breast in all its unencumbered beauty spurred me on.

I unbuckled my belt and opened my pants. Tilting the monitor of my laptop downward a little so the cam pointed at my crotch, I took another deep breath and pushed my pants and underwear down.

"Very nice. You big"

"That's pretty much your doing, sweetheart," I said. "Your breast is beautiful!"

Jolene smiled and rotated her shoulder a few times, causing her breast to jiggle up and down. My erection became just a little more firm as she reached her hands around her back and took off her bra.

"You cum?"

Oh god! More of this and I just might. I could already feel the sweat beading up in my groin. I was glad the chair was only vinyl.

"Play with yourself," she said with a casual smile.

I had never masturbated in front of an audience. Not even Evelyn early on. She was always pretty conservative. Nothing 'kinky.' And to her, if it wasn't the missionary position, it was kinky.

Now, after that history, sitting here stroking my penis while a beautiful, naked young girl watched, well yes, even to me it seemed pretty kinky. Probably even *without* that history it would still seem kinky.

But it was also really exciting! This gorgeous girl seemed to be really interested in me, for whatever reason. I mean, don't get me wrong, I'm no rube. I'm certainly not an amateur where the internet is concerned. I don't get taken in by the Nigerian lawyers that send me e-mails stating that their client has died and left me a million dollars. Or by the e-mails telling me that Bill Gates will give me a lot of money just for forwarding the e-mail.

So yes, I had some suspicions in the back of my mind.

But maybe good looking Romanian men were hard to find. How would I know? I've never been there. All I knew was that while I was pleasuring myself in front of my computer, Jolene was slipping off her panties. After just a couple of minutes, that's all it took to push me over the edge. I grabbed a tissue and I was done.

She smiled as I sat there panting, catching my breath.

And I heard footsteps on the stairs!

In a panic, I pulled my pants up and buttoned my shirt. I caught the briefest glimpse of the confusion on Jolene's face as I did this. I was behind my desk, so when Evelyn opened the door and looked in, the fact that my pants were still unzipped and my belt buckle hanging loose escaped her notice.

"I'm going to bed now," she said in a monotone.

"Okay," I said. I was concentrating on breathing slow and even, so that I wasn't panting. Evelyn looked at me oddly, then closed the door.

What the hell was that about? She never bothers to let me know when she's going to bed. Had I given off some kind of suspicious vibe that she had picked up on? Some kind of pervert pheromone? Whatever it was, I finished doing up my pants and pushed the monitor back up a bit so the cam was aimed at my face.

Jolene was waiting for me.

"What's wrong?"

"My wife just stuck her head in my den. I almost got caught!"

Jolene smiled.

"We alright now?"

I looked at her for a moment, feeling torn. Jolene was totally naked, and was completely comfortable with that. She was young and flawless, and seeing her so happily displaying her naked body to me was admittedly appealing.

"No," I replied. "I'm done. I need to get to bed anyway. Goodnight, Jolene."

I didn't wait for her to respond. I closed Yahoo Messenger and shut down my computer.

Shit, that was close! My heart was still pounding. I couldn't believe how near I had come to getting caught.

I took one final deep breath and let it out slowly as I stood up. As the adrenaline finally started running its course, I was able to breathe easier. I felt nervous and tingly all over, and I realized that, in a way, it was a good feeling.

I left my den and went down the hallway toward my bathroom, the image of Jolene's perfect little body still fresh in my mind.

didn't do it," Lanelle said, her blonde curls drooping down around her face as she stood there with her head bowed. She was five years old.

"Lanelle," I said, exasperated, "there's nobody else here. Nobody else could have done that." We both looked at the crayon marks on the wall, and Lanelle's eyes were filling with tears. "Do you remember what I told you about lying?"

The curls bounced as she silently shook her head.

"When you lie," I sighed, "there are consequences." She looked up at me and I realized that she didn't know what that word meant. "It's like cause and effect."

Damn it!

"Okay, whenever you do something, it causes something else to happen. When you say something that isn't true, it makes Mommy and me sad. And that makes you sad, because we have to punish you."

She looked up at me with her lip quivering, the giant tears now tumbling off her eyelids. I looked at her little face and my big stupid heart melted.

I sighed again and took her into my arms.

Yeah, she understood consequences just fine.

I honestly don't remember much about Tuesday. I mean about work. I very clearly remember being completely distracted by thoughts about Jolene and her gorgeous little body being offered to me.

In the course of my life, I had seen plenty of naked women online, in movies, and magazines. But there was something different about this. I mean there was the physical part, which of course I was doing to myself. And it was good because, let's face it, I know myself pretty well. But somehow, seeing Jolene in real time and actually interacting with her made the experience much more intense.

So during that next day at work, I logged on to Facebook two or three times, when I had the time and the privacy. But Jolene wasn't on. Before that day, I can't remember when I had felt such a profound disappointment.

I knew I was hooked.

Just as well, though, I thought. I had work to do, and I had to concentrate on it, especially if I was going to have any chance of getting that Senior Art Director job. So I focused my attention on the jobs on my desk and did the very best work that I could do.

I was rewarded with the feeling that the day had flown by. Before I knew it, I was in my car and on my way home. It was windy, and I was fighting to keep my Beemer from wandering out of my lane. In the back of my mind, there were the ever-present thoughts of wondering what Evelyn was going to be like. But in the front of my mind, it was a whole different story. I was anxious to get back online.

My time with Evelyn also went by rather quickly, and uneventfully. I don't know if my indifference toward her played a part in that or not. But the fact was that I really didn't care what she had to say, and somehow, I ended up not saying anything that provoked her.

By the time I was in my den and plopped behind my computer, with the wind howling outside, it was only eight o'clock.

There was a message from Chaisang.

"Hello Arden my friend. How are you?"

I felt an unusual disinterest in her message.

"I'm fine, Chaisang. How are you?"

I was already looking to see if there was also a message from Jolene. There wasn't, but I saw that she was online. I quickly sent her a message.

"Hi, Jolene. How are you doing?" Seemed like a tame enough contact.

"I fine Arden," came a response from Chaisang. "Is good to see you here, my friend."

"hi" was the response from Jolene.

Two very different chats at once. This could be dangerous.

"Thank you, Chaisang," I replied without asking any further questions.

"What are you doing, Jolene?" I asked in the other chat window.

"working" she replied.

"Oh, what do you do?"

Her response was simply a hyperlink.

"www.slut-chat.com" I clicked on the link and was taken to a site populated by countless girls in various states of undress, chatting with subscribers.

Huh.

"Slut chat?" I inquired. "I don't understand."

"What are you doing my friend?" was Chaisang's response. Unfortunately, I didn't feel like carrying on my usual 'relationship' with her. I had little interest in it any longer. So I ignored her.

"you sign up, you see me" was Jolene's reply.

So Jolene was one of the 'sluts' at Slut Chat, performing naked in front of a group of drooling, dirty old men?

The irony of the last part of that sentence escaped me at the time.

"What about last night?" I asked.

"last night was freebie. sign up you see more"

I didn't see myself in that audience. One on one with Jolene, that was different. That stroked my ego. Among other things. But sitting shoulder to virtual shoulder with several other men typing in requests of what they wanted to see her do, that just seemed dirty. And kind of sad.

Her icon disappeared from the right column of Facebook and I knew that she had gone offline. And just like that, it was over between Jolene and me.

"You still there Arden?" I looked at Chaisang's message and sighed.

"Yes, Chaisang, I'm here," I typed. "I'm not doing much. Just wishing you weren't so far away." I'm not sure where that came from.

"Why?"

"Because I'd love to see you in person, to be able to touch you."

The pause in the conversation left me wondering what she was thinking.

"But you marriage."

"Yes, I'm married," I said. "Sort of. I'm afraid it's not a good marriage."

"I sorry my friend. I not know you unhappy."

"I'm VERY unhappy. My wife and I are practically strangers. We haven't had sex in over a year. I miss the touch of a pretty girl."

"You wife pretty?"

Damn it! This girl completely missed the point! Couldn't she see that I didn't want to talk about my wife?

"She's kind of pretty. But we're not attracted to each other any longer."

"That sad, my dear friend."

"Yes, Chaisang, it's very sad. I wish I could be closer to you. I wish I could touch you and hold you."

"Mm yes, that would be nice my friend."

"You'd like that, Chaisang?" I asked her. "You'd like to hold me? You'd like to feel my arms around you?"

"Yes, my friend Arden. Nice to hold."

"Yes, very nice." My mind was racing now. "It would be so nice to feel your body against mine. To be able to run my fingers through your long hair. To lift your face and be able to kiss your lips."

"You want be my boyfriend?"

"I wish I could. You're such a beautiful young woman. I'd love to be able to be with you and make you happy."

"You do make me happy, my friend."

"I don't mean as a friend. I mean as a lover. I want to feel your skin against mine. I want to kiss you – your mouth, your breast, to make love to you."

"You don't want be my friend no more?"

"I want to be your friend, Chaisang. But I want to go beyond that. More than just friends. I want to be naked with you, loving you."

"But how?"

That simple, innocent question seemed to flip a switch and turn the sanity back on. How indeed?

"I don't know, Chaisang. I just wish." I paused in my typing and sighed. I belatedly started seeing the folly of what I was doing. Compared with my experience with Jolene last night, this was very unsatisfying. That's not to say that it couldn't become more satisfying. But did I even want it to? In the time that I had communicated with Chaisang, I had become close to her. I cared about her and her feelings. I realized that the attraction I had just been typing about was real.

And I felt guilty. Not toward my wife – I barely had any feelings for her any longer. I felt guilty toward Chaisang. A sweet, beautiful, innocent girl who had never given any indication that she wanted anything from me other than to be my friend. I felt as if I had betrayed her and our friendship.

But I also felt unmotivated to continue the friendship. To my credit, I at least felt enough for Chaisang to care about how she felt. So what I embarked upon next was in an effort to spare her feelings.

"I'm sorry, Chaisang. Maybe we should not be friends anymore. Wanting you, wishing I could hold you, it only makes it harder to find any happiness in my marriage." That ship had already sailed a long time ago, but for the point of the argument . . . .

"But I be sad if we not friends."

"I will be sad, too. But I think it's for the best."

"No, I not have good friends here in Thailand. You and me we talk like friends. We just not be lovers cause you marriage."

"I can't, Chaisang. I'll see you here on Facebook, and if we start talking, I'll just want to hold you and make love to you."

"You make me sad Arden. I want see my good friend."

"I'm sad too, Chaisang. I'm crying now." God, was she really buying all this? "I can't see you here or I'll be even more sad. Good bye, my sweet little friend."

I quickly moved my mouse to hover over her name. I clicked on the link to unfriend her. And just like that, I had cut it off with her.

I was a little surprised at how quickly this whole thing with Chaisang had progressed. Just yesterday, we were chatting about her life in Thailand, her family, her upcoming birthday. Then last night was my sexual encounter with Jolene, which introduced a new facet to my online world. And as an indirect result of that, I fucked everything up with Chaisang by introducing this romantic angle.

Actually, erotic would be more accurate, but as far as Chaisang knew, it was romantic.

And I felt a new guilt, now. I felt guilty for lying to Chaisang, telling her that I loved her. But our conversations just seemed kind of pointless to me now. Mundane. I honestly didn't really care about life in Thailand.

And I thought that telling Chaisang that I loved her would make her feel better than if I just stopped responding. I did it for her.

That's what I told myself, anyway.

On a summer afternoon, Evelyn and I lounged on the patio in back of our house. Since the back yard was on the north side of the house, we were shaded from the sun, so even though it was warm, we were pretty comfortable.

We were relaxed enough that we were actually enjoying each other's company. Or at least we were enjoying each other's silence.

Cicadas were buzzing in the trees, and seven year old Lanelle was crouched down in the grass, intently studying something. I took a sip of iced tea as I watched her.

"What are you doing, Lanelle?" Evelyn asked. Lanelle looked up briefly, her face screwed up in confusion. Then she looked back down again.

"These two grasshoppers are stuck together," she said. "One's standing on top of the other one."

I quickly pulled the glass away from my mouth as I attempted to keep from sputtering my iced tea. From the corner of my eye, I caught the look that Evelyn shot toward me.

"What are they doing?" Lanelle finally asked.

Evelyn seemed kind of flustered.

"One of them probably has a hurt leg," she said. "The other one is just giving him a piggyback ride."

I glanced at her, then back at Lanelle.

"Well," I countered, "that's not exactly what they're doing."

Lanelle looked up at me. "They're making baby grasshoppers."

Her face broke into a big smile as she looked back down at the humping hoppers.

"You can't tell her they're having sex!" Evelyn said under her breath.

"Well, that's not quite what I said. But I want her to know the truth instead of some cute little lie."

"She's too young to know about that."

"You think at least some of her friends don't know the truth?" I asked. "What if the subject comes up among them and Lanelle tells them that one grasshopper is just giving the other one a ride? Think about how she will probably be made fun of by the others who know. You want to put her through that?"

Evelyn turned away in disgust and shook her head.

I didn't care. I was enjoying watching the delight on Lanelle's face as she watched the grasshoppers.

Wednesday morning, the sky was a bright crystal blue. It was a cold but beautiful day. Yes, Jolene had turned out to be a professional slut and had 'dumped' me, but I had also broken it off with Chaisang. It seemed as if things were looking up.

What the hell did I know?

Evelyn woke up before I left for work, which was unusual. I was almost always gone by the time she got up. But Wednesday, when I was already running a little late, she hauled her carcass out of bed early enough to give me shit.

"What the hell is this?" she asked as I came back into the kitchen. I had just brushed my teeth and had come back downstairs and put my coat on. She was standing in the kitchen like a goddess, with her hair flattened on one side and a crust of dried drool on her face.

"What the hell is what?" I asked.

She pointed to the countertop. I looked at the indicated area and saw nothing, until I leaned in a little closer. There were some crumbs there where I had quickly eaten some toast for breakfast. I brushed them off into my hand and then into the sink.

"We've talked about this," she scolded.

"I know," I replied, hoping to be able to get away before we started the day with one of our epic arguments. "I'm sorry. I don't mean to be such a troglodyte."

"I work hard to keep this place looking nice," she began, "and you have agreed to help out a little." I turned on the faucet and washed away the offending detritus. I made a point of gesturing to the drain to show her that the crumbs were indeed no longer an obstacle to her happiness.

"I have to go," I said.

I managed to tear myself away from her and was now running even later. My usual routine when I get to work is to get a cup of coffee, settle into my chair and peruse Facebook for a few minutes before I jump into my work. But since I was about ten minutes late, I didn't have a chance until later in the morning, after Joe stuck his head in my office.

"What the hell have you been up to on Facebook?"

"What do you mean?" I asked. "I haven't been on."

"Looks like you've been up to no good," he said with his signature crooked smile. "It's kind of pitiful, but at the same time, I have to admit, I'm a little impressed."

I sat there looking up at him like an idiot. Joe was a Facebook friend, but we had little interaction online. He sometimes liked something I posted, and vice versa. But he'd never told me he was impressed by anything. I couldn't think of what he could be referring to. I still looked at Joe, my face screwed up in confusion.

"Well," he said with a typical sarcastic edge, "I've enjoyed this little talk of ours, but I have something interesting to get to." Then he left and closed the door.

Curious about what he was talking about, I cast a quick glance at the pile of work on my desk, then quickly turned to my computer and brought up Facebook.

I had several notifications waiting for me. Messages from friends who knew me pretty well. Baffling messages. "What the hell is going on, Arden?" "Have you been hacked?" And one that said, "Way to go Romeo!"

Huh?

Then I saw a notification that someone had posted something on my profile page. Someone named Chaisang Pradchaphet.

Arden Chase: It would be so nice to feel your body against mine. To be able to run my fingers through your long hair. To lift your face and be able to kiss your lips.

Chaisang Pradchaphet: You want be my boyfriend?

Arden Chase: I wish I could. You're such a beautiful young woman. I'd love to be able to be with you and make you happy.

Chaisang Pradchaphet: You do make me happy, my friend.

Arden Chase: I don't mean as a friend. I mean as a lover. I want to feel your skin against mine. I want to kiss you – your mouth, your breast, to make love to you.

Chaisang Pradchaphet: You don't want be my friend no more?

Arden Chase: I want to be your friend, Chaisang. But I want to go beyond that. More than just friends. I want to be naked with you, loving you.

Chaisang Pradchaphet: But how?

Arden Chase: I don't know, Chaisang. I just wish. I'm sorry, Chaisang. Maybe we should not be friends anymore. Wanting you, wishing I could hold you, it only makes it harder to find any happiness in my marriage.

Chaisang Pradchaphet: But I be sad if we not friends.

Arden Chase: I will be sad, too. But I think it's for the best.

Chaisang Pradchaphet: No, I not have good friends here in Thailand. You and me we talk like friends. We just not be lovers cause you marriage.

Arden Chase: I can't, Chaisang. I'll see you here on Facebook, and if we start talking, I'll just want to hold you and make love to you.

Chaisang Pradchaphet: You make me sad Arden. I want see my good friend

Arden Chase: I'm sad too, Chaisang. I'm crying now. I can't see you here or I'll be even more sad. Good bye my sweet little friend.

Yeah, that sweet little friend, that innocent waif from Thailand, had copied and posted a transcript of our conversation on my profile page. Right there on my Timeline for everyone to see.

The little bitch!

I started to delete the post, but thought better of it. Instead, the first thing I did was to move the cursor and hover over Chaisang's name. When a menu of options popped up, I selected the link that allowed me to block her. Now, neither of us could see the other. Even if she did a search for me, my page would not show up. I realized I should have done that last night instead of just unfriending her.

Angry, I quickly deleted the post and sat there breathing like an obscene caller. With my brain in a whirl, I thought for a minute about all the friends who had seen the post. A few of whom were also Evelyn's friends.

Yeah, I really needed word of this getting back to Evelyn!

So I quickly posted an explanation.

"Yes, as some of you have guessed, I was hacked. I guess I'll have to adjust my privacy settings or something. But I apologize to anybody who might have been disturbed by the offending post on my timeline."

I had seen people post similar messages, so while I had never been hacked myself, I hoped this explanation would be believable enough. Within just a couple of minutes, several people had 'liked' my post, and a friend responded.

"Good to know, Arden. I thought you were going to have to change your name and go into hiding!"

And that's where the idea came from. I'm a little slow, so it took a while to form, but when it did, I realized the

44

possibilities that presented themselves. I tried to keep my attention on my work that afternoon, but the idea was so intriguing, it kept pushing its way to the front of my mind.

* * *

Now let me just say right here that I'm not a dirty old man. I don't lust after women and spend all my waking hours thinking about sex.

But I *am* a man. A married man who should be getting it at home once in a while.

So as I was on the road that evening, I was working out the details in my mind. As I approached my house, I was spurred on even more by the sight of Cyndi Shelton next door. She was in her front yard gathering up a few twigs and branches that had littered her lawn from the wind the night before.

And despite the insulated jacket she wore, she still managed to look incredibly sexy.

Cyndi's house was smaller than mine, but it was still nice. Aside from a Springer Spaniel named Louie, she lived alone in her antique-furnished home. A home made possible in part by a sizable divorce settlement and hefty alimony payments from her cheating scumbag of an ex-husband.

Cyndi was the owner of Cater Tots, a small catering company that focused on children's events. Her claim to fame was her almost uncanny ability to make nutritious, grown-up style dishes palatable enough to children's tastes that she was in demand, not only here in Boulder, but as far north as Fort Collins and Estes Park, maybe even closer to the Wyoming border, and down into Denver, and all points in between.

After her separation from her husband eight years earlier, she had started the company for a little extra money, as a way to make ends meet. Working only on weekends, in a few months' time, the ends met, then overlapped. In time she was busy enough that she quit her office job and started catering full-time. Add that to the divorce settlement and alimony, and Cyndi was doing pretty well.

Tired of working in her cramped apartment in north Denver, she purchased her house five years ago. The house was a very cool mid-century modern structure, reminiscent of a Frank Lloyd Wright, surrounded by welcoming flower gardens, and only a few steps from a walking path that led eventually to the Flatirons. Having enlarged the kitchen, she now had a workspace large enough for her growing business.

Not that I had ever seen it. We had invited her over, along with several other neighbors, for a barbeque a couple of years back. But Evelyn spent the whole barbeque avoiding her when she could, and being cool to her when she couldn't, and remarked to me later that night that Cyndi looked like the neighborhood whore – because she wore some dark eyeliner and shorts. It was July, for God's sake, and others were wearing shorts too, though admittedly nobody else wore them as well as Cyndi did. Well, that was the last official contact that we had with her. I had never been in her house. I had to be satisfied with getting a glimpse of her in her front yard, or the occasional brief conversations over the fence.

She waved at me now as I drove past. I waved back and pressed the button on my garage door remote, keeping my eye on her as she made her way back into her house.

* * *

"What were you staring at?" was Evelyn's first remark to me as I walked in the door.

"Huh?"

"I saw you as you were driving up. You were staring at someone and you waved. Were you ogling the little slut next door?"

"Don't you have anything better to do?" I asked. When will I learn?

Evelyn glared at me and I knew what was coming.

She had never thought that she was very attractive and the years had not been kind. Her mother had always had a classic look about her, but Evelyn lamented that she had gotten her looks from her father. Actually, she had some decent features, but put together in combination, she just didn't like the way she looked.

Her mother had been domineering with Evelyn, even insulting at times, and that just served to reinforce her already poor self-image. Evelyn knew that she had been more attractive when she was younger, attractive enough for me to want to marry her. But the attraction was obviously long gone now.

"You used to give me compliments," she said.

"I still do."

"Rarely," she said with a look of disgust in her eyes, "and usually only after I ask you how I look."

I rolled my eyes but managed to keep my mouth shut.

"Compliments given when I prompt you for them don't count."

"What does that have to do with you watching me as I drive up?" I asked.

"I don't imagine Cyndi Shelton would have to prompt you for compliments." There was a particular edge to her voice as she said Cyndi's name.

"Oh my god," I said under my breath as I turned and looked out the front window. I just shook my head and shrugged my coat off. A sigh escaped my lips as I hung it up in the closet.

"So what's wrong now?" Evelyn asked.

"What do you mean?"

"You always seem to come home with some kind of problem. And you're cold to me and ignore me, and you usually blame it on your job."

"It's a stressful job," I said noncommittally. I knew better than to say anything about *her*.

"Then why don't you leave?"

"How am I supposed to leave my job? I have to pay for this house. And for all your name brand shit."

"I know, it's always my fault," she said with her sarcastic tone. I think I allowed my eyes to roll a little at that point. "I'm not the only one who wanted this house. And so what if I like nice things?"

"Well, there you have it," I said. "That's why I can't leave my job."

"You can get another one!"

"Yeah, because good jobs are so easy to come by."

"They're out there. You can't get it if you don't look."

"After my promotion and my raises, I'm not going to find another one that pays what I'm making now."

"So it's my fault that you're stressed out?"

"I never said it was your fault!"

"You usually imply that I'm part of the problem."

"How did I do that?" I asked. "I said absolutely nothing about you. Or about my job, until you asked."

"That was my point. You never say anything about me. Especially since that little whore moved in next door."

"Oh my god," I said again. I was getting dizzy from her circular logic.

"You often work late, and when you're home, you have no interest in me. But you sure are interested in Cyndi Shelton!" Again, she used that tone. And apparently the tone wasn't possible without a sneer on her face. "I've seen how you act when she's around. You act like a little puppy practically peeing on yourself to get near her. You're more interested in doing yard work than you ever were before."

"So we have a nice yard," I fired back sarcastically. "I know how you like a well-manicured lawn. You should be happy about that."

"You bastard," she said. "Are you fucking that little whore?"

"Oh shit," I sighed. "No, Evelyn, there is nothing going on between Cyndi and me."

"So, you're on a first name basis with her."

"Yes, I'm on a first name basis with our next door neighbor! God, how will we *ever* survive the scandal?"

"You son of a bitch," she spat at me. "You can get your own damn dinner. Just leave me alone!"

"I'm not hungry," I said casually over my shoulder, and I headed upstairs. The 'discussion' was shorter than usual, though I knew there was always the likelihood that Evelyn would pick it up later.

So I was actually settled at my computer by six-thirty and I opened up Facebook. I had it set so that it would automatically keep me logged in, so I found the link to log out. After it took me to the login page, I got ready to initiate my plan.

I had written some short stories when I was younger, though I had never done anything with them. A character in one of those stories was named Augustine Smith. This was the name I had decided to use. I clicked the link to sign up with Facebook as a new user, and I typed 'augustinesmith' as the user name. I created a password that was easy to remember, filled in other information that was asked for, and clicked Register.

And a message popped up stating that an account already existed for my e-mail address. Oopsie. I realized that I needed to use a different e-mail address. I thought about using my work address, but I decided that I didn't want to risk anything scandalous showing up in my in-box at work.

So I went to yahoo.com and clicked on the mail icon. I spent a couple of minutes there creating a new e-mail account with the name augustinesmith. Then I went back to Facebook and registered with the new e-mail address, entering all the necessary information.

And I got another message that said that Facebook recognized my phone number as being connected to another account that already existed.

Damn! Really?

I thought about it for a bit, but I couldn't think of how to get around Facebook's security measures. I knew it happened all the time. I've heard of people creating spurious Facebook accounts, to bilk people out of money, or for whatever reason people do it. Including scamming women. But apparently I wasn't technically savvy enough to know how to do that.

So I stopped thinking about it. I pulled some work out from the small briefcase that I took to my job with me and directed my attention to that.

When Evelyn surprised me by barging into my den about an hour later, I was making notes on a comp for a print ad campaign for a local microbrew. The fact that I always hear her approaching my den but didn't this time, as well as the expression that I took as a look of disappointment that flashed briefly across her face, told me she expected to catch me doing something wrong.

"What are you doing?" she asked.

"I'm *trying* to work. Why?"

She shook her head and sneered at me.

"You don't give a shit about me."

A favorite line of hers.

"You're wrong, Evelyn. I give plenty of shits about you."

"Why do you stay around? Why don't you just leave?"

"And what would you do if I left? How would you ever pay for this place?"

I know I was kind of on shaky ground with a question like that. Since her parents were pretty loaded, they could probably help her out. Still, though, she never had an answer for it, so I took advantage of the pause that ensued.

"Could you close the door, please?" I said. "I'm kind of busy."

She sneered at me again and slammed the door. I could hear her stomping away toward her bedroom, where I heard another slam.

* * *

You're probably wondering the same thing Evelyn did. Why did I stay around? Why didn't I just leave?

Like I already said, I stuck it out all those years for Lanelle. But now that she'd been gone to college for a few months, why didn't I just clear out? Or better yet, kick Evelyn's lazy ass out of the place?

Good questions.

The fact is, I don't know. The only plausible answer I can think of is that maybe all those years, I just grew accustomed to the way things were. I'm a creature of habit, and I am most comfortable with routines. So the routine I had settled in, unhealthy and unhappy as it was, was my comfort zone, to use the psychobabble vernacular so popular nowadays. Our relationship, defined by years of indifference, and punctuated by outbursts of hatred and anger, had been endured for so long that it had just become our lives.

Old habits are hard to break.

But I didn't think about it then. I finished up what I was working on, spent a little time browsing on Facebook, then went to bed.

He's a shithead!" Lanelle spat. "I hate him!" She said it with a bit more vitriol than I would have expected from a cute little nine year old girl.

"Honey, what have we told you about saying words like that?" I asked with my most authoritative father voice.

"You and Mom say it all the time!" she accused. She was right, but still . . . .

"Okay," I replied, "I know it seems like a double standard. And maybe it is, but sometimes grownups say things that kids shouldn't."

"But why? That's not fair!"

"I know, and I'm sorry, but that's the way it is." I stopped short of saying 'because I said so.' But Lanelle still wasn't happy with my explanation. I couldn't blame her. I guess I wouldn't have been either.

Damn! Kids are hard. But I tried to get back on topic.

"Now what about this boy?"

"What boy?" she asked.

"The one – " She hadn't told me anything about him yet, including his name, or why she was so mad at him. I sighed. "The shithead."

Her face pinched up in anger.

"Bobby Snyder. He's so gross!"

"Why? What did he do?"

"He kissed me!"
"He – "
That little shithead!

Having gotten to bed a little bit early the night before, I felt rested on Thursday morning and had gotten to work a few minutes earlier than usual. So as I sipped my coffee and browsed my Facebook notifications, the thought occurred to me that maybe I could just opt out of entering a phone number when I set up a new account.

Wondering if that would be all it would take, I logged out and repeated my actions of the night before. I created a Facebook account under the name Augustine Smith, using the augustinesmith Yahoo e-mail address. I didn't know if it would allow me to not enter a phone number, and I was holding my breath for a moment. When I got to that part, I skipped the phone number, and I was rewarded with a welcome page from Facebook. Now I needed to find photos to put on my profile page.

Now, I didn't want to use my own photographs. I had created a completely new identity to hide behind, so the pictures needed to be different too. Augustine Smith was a handsome single man, about ten years younger than me, whose biographical information was based on that short story that I had written years ago. So the photographs had to be of someone else, someone who looked about thirty-nine years old, and preferably a good-looking young man. I *did* want to attract good-looking women after all.

I did an image search at Yahoo for handsome young men and found three photographs that might be usable. They were most likely three different people, but I thought that, since they were from different angles with different lighting, they could conceivably be pictures of the same person.

Something bothered me about them, though. I couldn't say what. It was just like a tickle in the back of my brain that I couldn't reach.

Well, I couldn't figure out what it was, so I let it go. I wasn't finding that many pictures of good-looking young men in the right age group, with features similar enough that they could be the same person, so fuck it.

I uploaded them to the new, spurious account, along with a photo of the Boston skyline for the cover photo, since Augustine lived in Boston. I began filling in the personal information on the profile page, and eventually, Augustine became fleshed out into a real person.

Now, to find some friends for Augustine. There were a few friends on my personal Facebook account that were, frankly, a mystery to me. I don't remember how I ever got them. They had no known connection to my other friends, or to pages that I had liked. Erotic romance authors? I had never bought or read erotic romance novels. So how did they ever end up in my list of Facebook friends?

I didn't know, but they seemed like a good place to start. I looked up their names and found them, sending a friend request to each of them. Then I looked at *their* friends list, finding some intriguing possibilities. Good-looking, sexually outspoken women. They posted sexy pictures, suggestive memes, blurbs of erotic poetry.

I sent out friend requests to them too.

While I was at it, I made comments on some of the things they posted. I wanted to get Augustine out there, let

55

him be seen. Establish him as a real person, expressing a real personality. I 'liked' some of the sexual memes they posted, sometimes responding with a suggestive reply of my own.

Then, I thought of Chaisang. I already knew that I liked her, at least before I, Arden, had upset her and she posted our conversation on my page. She hadn't really balked at the idea of a sexual relationship. I just didn't want her connected to my own friends, or to have access to my page. But Augustine had no relation to me. Arden Chase in Boulder, Colorado had no connection whatsoever to Augustine Smith in Boston, Massachusetts.

So, as Augustine, I sent a friend request to Chaisang as well.

I heard voices outside my door, which brought me back to the present. I realized that time had sped past and it was well after when I should have started working. I minimized my web browser and got to work.

I'm sure that, by now, you're probably thinking what a jerk I am. And I don't know, maybe I am. But like I said earlier, I'm an able-bodied man who hadn't had sex in over a year. Having experienced the excitement of e-sex just a couple of nights ago with Jolene, I felt like I needed a little outlet, and this seemed like a harmless way to do it.

But I didn't trouble myself with how others might see me for doing this. I didn't care, because nobody would know. That was the whole point – anonymity.

I was busy all morning and ended up taking a late lunch, at which time I went back into Facebook, where Augustine's account was still open. And I – he – had gained seven friends, and had actually received several friend requests from other people. I didn't know why. Augustine had not even posted anything of his own yet, and had only minimal information on his profile page. But it was fine with me. I approved all the requests.

A couple of them were friends of the erotic authors, but I had no idea where the others had come from. Several were young girls in India, Pakistan, Bangladesh, the Philippines. How they ever found Augustine, I don't know.

One of the new friends was Chaisang. She had accepted the friend request I had sent.

I made it a point to send a personal message to her.

"Hi Chaisang. Thanks for accepting my friend request."

I just left it at that. Plain and simple.

Then I spent a little time perusing the profiles of my new friends. Yes, *my* new friends, because I was beginning to think of myself as Augustine Smith. I looked at the photographs that they had uploaded, especially the good-looking women. I looked at their friend lists, and sent out more requests.

And that was when I found JuleighAnn. JuleighAnn Harper. An absolutely beautiful woman in Lakewood, Colorado of all places, a western suburb of Denver.

JuleighAnn was a talented woman of forty. She was an amateur photographer with an incredibly artistic eye. She posted moody-looking photographs, often captioned with poetic or philosophical verses. The pictures she took around her neighborhood were beautiful, kind of dark and melancholy, but what especially captivated me were the photos she took of herself.

In some of them, she was wearing makeup – a dark smoky effect with a soft focus. Others were without makeup, and those were beautiful as well. Some were by herself, others with her dog. But her eyes drew me in and her adorable, good-natured smile held me tight.

I sent a friend request.

By that time, I had exceeded my lunch time, so I minimized the browser and went back to work again.

* * *

Late afternoon, I checked in again and found that I had gotten a few more new friends. I was a little impatient, though, that JuleighAnn Harper was not one of them yet. I found her profile page again and took the opportunity to look at a few of her profile pictures, and I had one of my favorites up on the screen for a few moments.

Her face was gentle, her lips curved ever so slightly in a smile that transmitted, not so much mirth, but mischief. Her hair was very dark, a brown just this side of black.

But her eyes were what held me. They were a soft golden green, warm, and seemed to be illuminated by an amber light behind them. The corners of her eyes were faintly crinkled in just the beginnings of a smile, as if they were seconding the mischief on her lips.

"Good god!" came Joe's voice from behind me. "Who is that gorgeous creature?"

I jumped a little, surprised. I hadn't heard my door open. I turned, and made no pretense since I knew it was too late to hide the browser.

As Joe was alone, I motioned him into my office. He closed the door behind him and came toward my computer, his eyes still glued to the monitor. Knowing Joe's lustful weakness for beautiful women, I decided that my best option was to just tell the truth. If anybody would appreciate my plan, he would.

"I'm conducting something of an experiment," I said. "I've created a new identity on Facebook to troll for beautiful women."

"Yeah, well I think you've caught one," he said, looking at JuleighAnn.

I looked back at the picture, appreciating the beauty that had now captured Joe as well.

"Wait," he said, the spell apparently being broken as he realized what I had said. "Trolling for beautiful women? What are you talking about?"

I was a little embarrassed, but I decided to tell Joe about my encounter with Jolene the other night. As I related the experience, I could see that Joe was enjoying it. To the point where he sputtered a little as I told how Evelyn walked in on me. And he displayed his crooked smile when I told about Chaisang posting our conversation on my profile page.

"So," I continued, "I decided that I would try creating a new profile, an assumed identity, and play around with that."

"I don't blame you, man," Joe said. "I don't know how you've held out *this* long." A couple of years ago, over a few beers after work, I had revealed to him what my relationship with Evelyn was like. Even back then, Evelyn and I had sex only about once every several months, whether we needed to or not. "I would have been out of there years ago and put myself back on the market!"

"I know," I said. I looked back at JuleighAnn's picture on the screen.

"So, Augustine Smith," Joe said. "Good luck with that. Maybe you'll find Miss Right on there." He paused, then brightened a bit, as if remembering something. "Oh anyway, the reason I came in here, a few of us are going out to Rock Bottom for a drink after work."

Rock Bottom Brewery was a favorite after-work gathering place. I loved their beers, and their nachos. I looked at my watch. It was after four o'clock.

"Evelyn's probably got dinner started by now," I said. "After our most recent blow-up, I probably shouldn't rock the boat. So I think I'll pass this time."

"Okay, man," Joe said, shaking his head a little. "Suit yourself." He went toward the door and opened it. "You should get yourself out of there," he said in a high, sing-songy voice.

He left and closed the door, leaving me pondering JuleighAnn's photo.

* * *

About a half hour later, Ed Leeson, my boss, came into my office. Fortunately, I had finished drooling over JuleighAnn Harper's picture by then and was actually working.

"Arden," he said, "we have something of a situation. Melanie is apparently experiencing a bit of a block with the MaxiMed ad." Ed dropped himself into the chair in front of my desk.

Melanie Evans was one of our best creatives, an imaginative artist with a good eye for detail and a background in fantasy illustration. Before she had come to work for Argosy, she had actually published a couple of children's books that she had written and illustrated herself. She regularly teamed with Bob Tennant, and together, they had pumped out some of Argosy's best work in recent years.

"What's the problem?" I asked.

"She says she's just not feeling it. I mean, she didn't tell *me* that. That's what Bob said. But he agreed that they're both having some trouble with it. Frankly, I think it's just a coincidence of dynamics. She's in the middle of moving, and he's worried about his wife." Harley Tennant had been battling ovarian cancer and seemed to be losing.

"They're both distracted," I said.

"Exactly." Ed shifted in his chair, sitting up a little straighter, and quickly sucked in a breath as he sometimes did to signal that he was coming to the point. He looked down at the file folder he was holding. "So, I was wondering if you could take a look at it. See if you can come up with a good angle. Maybe get them started." He glanced at the Addies on my shelf. "Or, maybe if you have the time, you could carry this one."

"You mean be a creative again for this job?" Ed nodded. "Absolutely! I'd be happy to."

He smiled and handed me the folder.

"Bob and Melanie put together what they had. A couple of pencil sketches from Melanie, and there's a flash drive in there with some doodles Bob did in Illustrator. Not much, really, but it's a start."

"I'll see what I can do."

"Great!" Ed said as he hauled himself out of the chair. "Good luck, Arden."

I was already looking at the material and didn't even notice him leaving. Maximum Medical Protection, Inc., or

MaxiMed, was a Denver-based company that provided in-home care to elderly and chronically ill patients. Due to the general public's increasing distaste for corporations, MaxiMed wanted, instead, to be portrayed as regular folks. They hoped to draw attention to the personalized care they gave to each individual client, and they wanted an ad campaign to show them as real people.

They had stumbled several months ago when numerous patients had been given incorrect medications, or incorrect dosages, resulting in illness and even two wrongful deaths. MaxiMed was in the news daily as the investigation went on, followed by the class-action lawsuit, as well as a few individual civil suits.

The situation had finally been rectified when the caregiver responsible was arrested. Turns out he had falsified his resume to get the job, and the person who had hired him was severely disciplined for not checking his references. MaxiMed ultimately paid out millions of dollars in judgments. Hoping now to regain the trust of the public, they had hired Argosy to boost their image as a caring group of people.

As I looked at the meager work in the folder, it occurred to me that maybe Bob Tennant was not the best person to be working on a medical account, given the situation with his wife.

And in a further burst of insight, I remembered that Melanie was in the process of moving because of the chronic illness of her husband. Mitch Evans had myasthenia gravis and was on disability. Since he was unable to work, they couldn't afford their house any longer on just her salary, so they were downsizing into an apartment.

Both of them were being influenced in some way by the health-care system. One way or another, their objectivity was affected, so it was no wonder this was a difficult account for them.

I looked over the notes and other paperwork on MaxiMed's objective. A few ideas started swirling in my mind, and it was after five before I noticed what time it was. I packed everything up and left for the day.

* * *

The drive home was longer than usual. There was an accident on 36, the highway commonly known as the Boulder Turnpike, and traffic had slowed to a crawl. I had plenty of time to think, and my thoughts were a befuddled mix of beautiful new Facebook friends and MaxiMed propaganda.

While I was on my way home, I called Evelyn to let her know I was going to be later than usual, only to find that she wasn't at home anyway. She was out shopping. Retail therapy seemed to help when she was angry or depressed. So despite the resentment I felt about her need to spend my money, I was hoping that she might actually be in a good mood. Rather than expecting her to cook when she got home, I offered to pick up some food from a little Thai restaurant that I knew she liked.

It was nearly seven o'clock when I got home. By that time, Evelyn was home as well, and she spent a few minutes happily showing me the blouses and shoes that she had bought. I was happy for her, because she actually seemed happy herself. Which tonight was good for me, so I was also happy for myself.

Dinner was fairly quiet, but the mood was good. We talked a little about our days – not *too* much because she had little interest in or understanding of what I did, and I didn't really care much about her shopping expedition either. But the time was passed comfortably. And having told Evelyn about being given the MaxiMed account, the groundwork was laid for my excusing myself to go to work in my den.

By eight o'clock, I had the MaxiMed material spread out on my desk. I fired up my computer and, well, just to get it out of the way, I decided to check Facebook first. There were a few notifications on my personal account. Then I logged out, after which I logged back in as Augustine Smith.

I had several friend approvals, and a few friend requests. And there was a personal message from Chaisang, a response to my greeting.

"Hello my new friend Augustine. Its nice to meet you."

"Very nice to meet you too, Chaisang," I replied. "You can call me Gus." I thought that was a good touch. Somebody named Augustine would likely use a nickname, something shorter. I can be kind of bright sometimes.

"Hello Gus," she responded almost immediately. She was online now. "Where you live?"

Doesn't anybody look at profile pages?

"I'm in Boulder," I typed. Then I remembered that I was online as Augustine Smith. Fortunately, I remembered this before sending the message. I backspaced through 'Boulder' and typed 'Boston, Massachusetts.'

I have to be more careful to not get my two identities confused.

"Im in Bangkok, Thailand," she replied. "What is weather like there?"

I was already getting bored with this. I didn't create an alternate identity to just engage in small talk. I didn't bother to check what the weather was like in Boston. I just said, "Cold."

I browsed my timeline, seeing things that others had posted. There were a lot of sexy one-liners and pictures posted by the erotic authors I had befriended, and I made it a point to like several of them, even giving brief responses to a few.

Then, I received a personal message from someone I had never heard of, a Robert Richardson.

"I use that avatar a lot in my class," he said. "The girls love it!"

What the hell?

I looked up Robert Richardson's profile page. He was a university professor in Indiana, and a friend of somebody that I had responded to. Then it sunk in what he was talking about. When I responded to a status update that he could see, that of a mutual friend, he saw Augustine's profile picture, his avatar. The one I found online.

He was letting me know that he knew it wasn't 'my' picture.

Shit!

I didn't bother to respond. I just deleted the picture and assigned one of the other two as the profile picture. I hoped nobody would notice, but I didn't think there was much chance of that, as new as Augustine's profile was.

As I had been dealing with the picture SNAFU, I received a couple of new notifications. One of my friend requests had been accepted. By JuleighAnn Harper. And I actually felt a little flutter in my chest when I saw that.

What the hell was that?

"Hi JuleighAnn," I immediately wrote to her. The sooner I made contact, the sooner she might respond. "Thank you for the friendship."

I meandered through her photographs again, lingering on a couple of them that really focused on her heartbreakingly beautiful face. Her jewel-like eyes just drew me in and wrapped themselves around me.

After a few minutes, and a few more messages with Chaisang, I realized that I was wasting time. I needed to work on the MaxiMed ad, so I said goodbye to Chaisang, minimized Facebook and plugged in the flash drive from Bob.

The sketches from Melanie, while typically refined, had unfortunately not been very helpful, and there was really nothing usable on the flash drive either. I was starting from scratch, which was fine with me. I reached up to a shelf and pulled down my sketch pad which had seen very little action in quite a long time.

Different creatives worked in different ways. Melanie could form complete pictures in her mind, and she liked to dash out fairly detailed drawings right from the beginning. She worked quickly on these initial drawings, so it worked for her.

While Bob was primarily a wordsmith, he had a bit of a background in graphics. He preferred to work electronically, blocking out shapes and text in Adobe Illustrator or Photoshop, then using those digital sketches as the basis for laying out his more detailed ideas.

I worked in kind of a combination of the two approaches. I liked to do it by hand, on paper, more detailed than Bob's rough geometric layouts, but not as detailed as Melanie' compositions.

I was busy putting a few ideas on paper when I heard the 'ping' that sounds when I receive a personal message in Facebook.

I pulled Facebook back up and saw that I had received a response to my introductory message to JuleighAnn Harper.

"Hi, Augustine. (Cool name!) Nice to meet you."

Okay Arden, remember now, you're Augustine Smith, in Boston.

"Thank you, JuleighAnn," I typed. "Very nice to meet you too. Augustine is kind of a long name to type, though. I usually go by Gus."

"Okay, Gus," she replied. "An alias, huh? Who are you hiding from?"

If you only knew! I didn't have a ready response.

"Well, JuleighAnn is kind of long too," she continued. "Some of my friends call me Jules."

"Jules," I typed. "I don't know. I like JuleighAnn. That's a very pretty name."

"Thanks. Sounds like you're buttering me up for something. What do you want?" But she followed that with a smiley.

Nice comeback! This chick was quick!

I thought about saying, 'I want to get in your virtual pants.' But I didn't. I didn't feel quite that safe with my anonymity yet. Plus, there was something about JuleighAnn. I didn't feel like going in that direction. Not yet, anyway.

But while I was busy musing over a snappy answer, she continued.

"So you're in Boston. Beautiful town!"

I liked this lady already. Besides being breathtakingly gorgeous and witty, she also had a head on her shoulders. She had the intelligence to know how to get information from a person's profile page, and the motivation to actually do it.

"Yes, it is," I replied. "I'm a transplant. Just moved here a few months ago."

Time to start creating Augustine in more depth. I had visited Boston a few years ago and loved it. Besides the artistic streak, part of what had made me nerdy in school was my love of history, a love that had stayed with me into adulthood.

When Ed and I went to Boston a few years ago to court a potential new client in the wake of my most recent Addy, I fell in love with the city. I loved how they preserved so much of their history instead of tearing it down to put up sterile, mundane glass skyscrapers.

I did all the touristy stuff I could fit into my free time there, including walking the Freedom Trail. Seeing the two hundred plus year old buildings that had figured in the American Revolution was thrilling to me.

And I had taken a ton of photographs, which I thought would help me in building Augustine's profile page now.

"I visited years ago," she said, "but haven't been back in a while. I loved it, though."

"So, Lakewood?" I typed. I figured that, across the country, Lakewood wouldn't be as well-known as, say, Denver. "Where is that in Colorado?"

"It's a western suburb of Denver," she replied. "I never really cared for suburbs until I found this nice little neighborhood around a lake. Feels like living in the country."

"Nice!" I said.

Yeah, I know, I needed to get to work on the MaxiMed job, but I was just enthralled with JuleighAnn and I couldn't tear myself away. To actually be conversing with this vision of loveliness, this person who made me use phrases like 'vision of loveliness,' was almost more than I could take.

During the next hour or more, I found out a lot about JuleighAnn.

"I grew up in a small town in Kansas," she said after I asked about her family. "My parents divorced when I was a little girl. I'm an only child, but my mother still had a hard time taking care of me. She had several bouts with cancer."

There was a pause. One of the hardest things about text messages is not knowing what the pauses mean. I didn't know if she expected me to give a response, or if she was just gathering her thoughts. Or if her dog knocked something over and she was just distracted.

I had just started to think about interjecting something when I saw that she had started typing again.

"She was into natural healing and tried all kinds of alternative treatments. They seemed to help for a while. But her body just became a tumor factory. She'd get one beat and she'd have another one show up somewhere else. By the time she relented and went to a medical doctor, it was too late. She was just too eaten up by the cancer."

"My God, JuleighAnn," I replied. "I'm so sorry."

"Yeah, it was bad. She lingered for a while. They tried to keep her comfortable at the hospital, but the last aggressive recurrence was just too advanced. She died about fifteen years ago. That was when I picked up and moved out here to Colorado."

I took another look at her picture and I pondered the inner strength that she must possess. To lose her mother and then to leave behind everything she knew to move to a new place all by herself showed me that she wasn't just a pretty face.

"So things were better for you in Colorado?" I typed.

"Well, no. Not initially, anyway. I met a man, Jack, who seemed like a great guy. He doted on me, complimented me, took care of me. We were in love, and I moved in with him.

"But after a while, he turned out to be very different than he had seemed at first. He drank quite a bit, and one time after he had gotten drunk, he beat me up. Bloodied my nose, busted my lip, left me with two black eyes and various other bruises."

"Oh my God! That bastard!" I looked at her picture again. I couldn't imagine someone doing that to that face.

"I moved out and I filed charges," she continued, "but he skipped bail and disappeared. I thought he'd gotten away with it until he showed up again a few years ago. That was when he beat up his latest conquest. I don't know how many he beat up between me and her, but she filed charges too. He didn't make it away that time. He's serving time in prison down in Cañon City."

"Good!" I replied. "I think it's pretty noteworthy that you moved out and pressed charges. I hear of so many

70

women who are afraid and stick around, only to get beaten over and over. I think it shows real strength on your part."

"Well, I'm just glad he's not beating women anymore. Maybe he's getting some of his own medicine now."

As we chatted, I continued looking through her photos, and I came to one that *really* caught my eye. She had her arms around her dog, a Golden Retriever, and JuleighAnn's smile was bigger and warmer than I had seen in any of the other photos.

"I just saw your picture with your dog," I said. "What a beautiful smile!" Then, as an afterthought, I added, "Yours is pretty nice, too." I grinned at my cleverness. I kept clicking through the photos of her and her dog, and I noticed a trend.

"Thank you," she replied.

"You know," I said, "I just realized that you seem to smile bigger in the pictures where you're with your dog."

"Yeah," she said, "Molson's my baby. He always seems to know what I need, and he's always there for me."

"You have a Golden Retriever named Molson?" I responded. "Okay, I thought I was clever, but you've outdone me."

The time passed and our conversation continued. And I learned more and more about her clever and subtle sense of humor, her creativity, and her strength. I learned all this and more about JuleighAnn.

Nothing about her favorite sexual position. Nothing about what she wears to bed. Nothing about what she yells out when she's having sex. Really, nothing at all that I created this fake identity for in the first place. But I was loving it.

71

Because I was loving her.

Yeah I know, it's ridiculous. I had never even seen this person face to face, and I only met her *online* a little over an hour before. As somebody else. How the hell could I be falling in love with her already?

I'll tell you how. My marriage was a joke. A joke without a punchline. Evelyn and I didn't hate each other. That would require more feeling or connection than we actually had. Instead, we were indifferent toward each other. The fights and anger, all the drama, just made it *feel* like there was something there.

But that was an illusion. There was nothing. We had nothing in common and we had both become lonely. Even when we were together, we were alone. The desolation was stifling. It was as if our voices were muffled even when we spoke face to face. We could be two feet apart but were separated by a bleak canyon, a vast distance of wasteland spread out between us.

And suddenly I find this creature who appealed, not only to my eyes but to my whole being. Her photographs of nature and of Denver showed me things that were familiar but different, because they were seen now through her eyes. And her self-portraits allowed me to see more than just a beautiful woman. In her face, her eyes, I saw her soul, and I connected with it in a way that I never had before. With anyone.

She inspired me.

And now it was 9:30 and I still hadn't done anything with MaxiMed.

"Well, JuleighAnn," I typed, "I hate to say it, but it's 11:30 and I need to get to bed if I'm going to be any good at work tomorrow." Fortunately, I remembered the two hour time difference between here and Boston.

"Okay, Gus. It's been very nice chatting with you. Thanks for connecting."

"Thank you, JuleighAnn. Good night."

I reluctantly moved the arrow up to the red "X" in the upper right corner of the chat window and closed it. And at that moment, I felt like an addict, strung out on the drug of his choice, and trying to stretch out his last buzz.

I sighed and looked at the MaxiMed material, and I got to work. Really. Because when I said that JuleighAnn inspired me, I meant it. Ideas were crystallizing, flowing through my fingers onto my sketch pad.

I thought about JuleighAnn's mother, her extended and painful illness, and how the poor woman had slowly and sadly wasted away in a cold and sterile hospital room. I moved from the sketch pad back to the computer and with faces I found online, I started putting together some quick comps.

It was nearly eleven o'clock when I quit for the night, but by that time, I had designed three very nice looking print ads, which I knew that MaxiMed would love.

I went to bed feeling more relaxed than I had in years.

When Lanelle was ten years old, she was sitting on the sofa in the living room by the fire. She was looking at something, but I couldn't tell what it was. She was sitting very still, her chin resting on one hand.

"She's been like that ever since she came home from school," Evelyn told me quietly from the doorway into the kitchen.

"Is something wrong?" I asked just as quietly.

"I don't know. She hasn't said anything."

"Did you ask her?"

Evelyn turned toward me and looked stern. "I don't want to encourage this moodiness," she replied indignantly. She turned and looked back at Lanelle. "She needs to deal with it and not spoil our evening."

"She's ten years old, Evelyn. For God's sake, lighten up."

I hadn't learned yet. I did later that evening.

I left Evelyn behind and went into the living room. Lanelle looked up at me as I approached.

"Hey, Lovebug," I said. "How's it going?"

"Okay," she said in a voice that didn't really invite believing.

"Yeah? What are you looking at?"

She turned it toward me a little. It was a school photograph, a group photo of her whole class.

"Oh, nice," I said as I took it and looked at it more closely.

I sat down beside Lanelle on the sofa, and she settled up next to me as I put one arm around her. I found her in the photo immediately. She was adorable, her blonde hair hanging past her shoulders, not as curly as when she was a toddler, though still just a little unruly.

But her big, happy smile was contagious. I smiled just looking at her.

"You look very pretty," I said. "As usual."

I looked down at her now, that smile noticeably absent from her face.

"So what's the matter, little one?"

She looked back down at the picture. She was hesitating. She acted as if she wanted to talk about something, but didn't quite know how to start. I waited, allowing her time to gather her thoughts.

"Boys are gross!" she finally blurted out, still looking at the photo.

"So I've heard."

She turned and looked up at me.

"Well, except you," she said quickly.

"Thank you," I said with a smile.

"But other boys are icky."

"I think that's a universally established fact."

Again, I waited. Finally she pointed to a boy in the picture, a good-looking little kid with dark hair and eyes.

"Then why do I think he's so cute?" she asked.

I smiled wistfully and held her a little closer.

I woke up Friday morning feeling unusually rested and refreshed. I'd like to say it was because I dreamed about JuleighAnn Harper. I don't think I did, but I'm sure she had something to do with it.

My drive to work seemed faster, the air was warmer, especially for December, the sky was bluer, and the sun a little brighter.

God, what the hell was wrong with me?

I got into my office and pulled out the comps that I had done the night before. In the light of day, they still looked great, and I knew it was going to be a good day. I settled at my computer with a cup of coffee and logged onto Facebook as Arden Chase. A few notifications awaited, but nothing terribly exciting.

Yeah, that sounded like me.

Then I logged in as Augustine Smith. There were numerous notifications and friend requests. Obviously, Augustine Smith was a much more interesting person than Arden Chase was. I looked at the friend requests first. A couple of girls from India, one from the Philippines, and a gorgeous blonde from Miami. They reminded me of what I had created this alternate identity for in the first place.

I approved them all.

Sipping my coffee, I breezed through the notifications, which were mostly funny memes, some of them pretty arousing. Damn, those erotic author ladies sure posted some sexy shit! Some of it downright pornographic!

Then I closed Facebook and got to work, with a little more enthusiasm, I think, than I had in a long time.

Ed wasn't in yet. He usually didn't show up until an hour or more after I did, so I started sifting through the work on my desk. But I was excited to show him what I had come up with on the MaxiMed account. It felt good to be creating again, and that feeling helped me through the stack of AD jobs I had to do.

I looked forward to having that feeling a lot more as Senior Art Director.

* * *

I didn't get a chance to talk to Ed until almost noon. I didn't notice when he came in since I was busy with my work for a while, looking at sketches and comps, talking with the creatives. Then I had a meeting with a client, and we were in the conference room with Mike Jellison, the current Senior Art Director, and the creative team for over an hour. By the time we got it wrapped up, Ed was getting ready to go to lunch.

"Ed," I said as I walked into his office, rapping on his open door. He was tugging his jacket on. I had the comps I had done on the MaxiMed account in a folder in my hand. "Could I talk to you for a minute?"

"Oh, Arden," he said. "Yeah, come on in. Sorry, I haven't had an opportunity to talk with you before now. Bob and Melanie told me they were able to work something out on MaxiMed after all. So you're off the hook."

"Wait, off the hook? I *wanted* to do it. And I've got some comps already. Really good ones!"

"Oh," he said. He really was a doink sometimes. "Well, Arden, it's their account. Go ahead and leave the comps with me. We can have them as backup. But I'll let them run with what they've got for now."

I just stood there looking at him like a moron. I thought of a thing or two to say, but I had the good sense to not say them.

"Was there something else?" he asked after my hesitation.

"No," I finally answered.

"Okay, good. I have a lunch meeting I need to get to. I do appreciate your willingness to help, Arden."

Then he left. Fucking bastard!

I dragged my feet back to my office and threw myself down in my chair. I had gotten a lot of work done that morning. Not to mention the work I did the night before on the MaxiMed job! No, I'm not letting go of that. But my point was that my work was caught up. So I turned to my computer and pulled up Facebook. I logged on as Augustine Smith and checked my notifications.

Once again, I had a couple of friend requests and one friend approval. And there was a personal message from an earlier one. The gorgeous blonde from Florida. Barbie Wilcox.

"Hi Augustine. Nice to meet you."

I opened up her profile page again. She only had one picture of herself, but she was beautiful! Not soft and accessible like JuleighAnn Harper. Barbie looked more like a model, with quite a bit of makeup, but as the saying went, 'I wouldn't kick her out of bed.'

"Hi Barbie. Very nice to meet you too. You can call me Gus." I looked in the column to the right and saw that she was online now. So her response came quickly.

"You're very handsome. Is that picture you?"

"Yes, it is," I lied. "You look pretty phenomenal yourself."

"Thanks. Too bad we don't live closer so we could get together."

Maybe *not* a bad thing since I don't look anything like my profile picture.

"I know," I replied. "I'd love to meet you in person."

We went on like that for over a half hour, exchanging tidbits of personal information, while at the same time tossing out subtle references to each other's looks. I had very little experience with sex chats, and the one experience I *did* have didn't end well. So I was taking it easy, wanting to introduce the subject, but afraid it might turn her off.

Barbie's comments were subtle too. Often suggestive, but never explicit.

That is until she dropped the bombshell.

"Oh god, I really need to be fucked!"

Well, that certainly eased us over the threshold.

"I can't imagine that would be very difficult, with the way you look," I replied, treading softly. "You sure wouldn't have to ask ME twice."

"Will you?"

Uh . . . .

"Will I what?" I asked stupidly.

"Fuck me."

I began to feel a curious swelling.

"Even at my most aroused, I don't think my penis would reach to Miami," I replied, smiling at my cleverness.

"Ohhh, too bad. You're a gorgeous man. I wish I could feel you inside me."

God, is this chick a nympho or what?

Not that I was complaining.

"I wish I could be inside you too, Barbie," I said. "But I'm at work right now. Maybe we should pick this up a little later."

"Okay," she responded. "About eight o'clock?"

A quick time-zone calculation and I knew that would be six o'clock in Colorado. I would probably be eating dinner then.

"Let's make it nine," I suggested. "I have some errands to run after work."

"I'll be waiting, Gus."

"Until then," I said, wanting to leave her with an appetizer, "rub your nipple and pretend it's me doing it."

"I'm rubbing my nipple right now, lover!"

I shook my head and smiled as I minimized the browser. I shifted in my chair, rearranging what Barbie had done to me.

* * *

"I'm going out with Maggie tomorrow," Evelyn said that evening at dinner. Maggie was sort of a friend.

"Great," I said, shoving another forkful of Salmon Alfredo in my mouth.

"Why is that great?" she asked me with a suspicious look on her face.

Careful . . .

"Just because you usually have a good time with her," I replied casually.

"Sometimes. She tends to be kind of arrogant."

Evelyn was an expert at finding the bad in others. I decided it might work out better to steer the conversation away from Maggie.

"I think it will do you good to get out for a little fun."

She nodded, and I concluded that I had successfully deflected an argument. I finished the last couple of bites and stood up.

"This was delicious," I said as a *coup-de-grace*, hoping to insure a trouble-free evening. Besides, it really *was* delicious.

"Thanks," Evelyn said. She almost seemed confused by my compliment.

"Well, I need to get to work," I said as I carried my dishes to the kitchen. I hadn't told her that Ed had shot down my creative opportunity. I figured I could still milk a little more mileage from it here at home.

Comfortably installed at my computer, I logged onto Facebook as Augustine. There was already a message from Barbie.

"Hi, lover. Can we do a video chat?"

Hmm. I don't look like Augustine, so I know that won't work.

"Sorry, Barbie. My web cam is on the fritz. I need to get it fixed or get a new one. We'll just have to do text for now."

"Oh, too bad, honey. I want us to see each other."

"What are you wanting to show me?" I asked, hopeful.

"I want us to make love!" she said.

"Well, we're a little far apart," I replied.

"My blouse is unbuttoned. I'm not wearing a bra. And I'm rubbing my nipple for you."

I don't think any editorial remarks are necessary here, do you?

"Sounds good," I typed. "I'm stroking my penis." And by that time, I was.

"Are you naked?"

"Not completely," I replied. Not at all, really, but I wasn't going to get caught in that trap again!

"I'm pulling my panties down. I'm so wet!"

"Yeah, I'm getting pretty damp too!"

I was. And apparently, my pants had shrunk. I decided it was time to get into the spirit.

"I'm leaning forward," I typed, "feeling your breasts pressed against my chest. Our naked bodies, skin to skin, press together, slippery with sweat. Our breathing speeds up as we move together."

Not bad! I could feel the shortness of breath that I had felt the other night, and I was really starting to get into this.

"You roll onto your back and I kiss your lips," I continue. "I cup my hand over your breast, loving the silky smoothness of it, and I bend over and kiss your nipple."

"I moan as your tongue traces the outline of my hardening nipple," Barbie replied.

"I move my hand down your body. You open your legs, inviting me in, and my fingers touch the soft fleshy lips of your vagina. I spread the lips apart and find the hard little button of your clitoris and begin rubbing it."

Now we're talking!

"I'm breathing harder," she said, "as you work your fingers up and down on my nub."

I was breathing harder, too.

"You reach down and touch my penis, and it responds, growing larger in your hand."

"I put my hands on your body and guide you up on top of me."

"Right where I want to be," I typed with a smile. "You take my penis, now fully erect in your hand, and guide it into your vagina. I slip inside you, and we both moan with the ecstasy of being so close, so warm. I move in and out of you, slowly at first."

"I wrap my legs around you, holding you tight."

"You arch your back, pressing against me harder, and I begin moving faster, still fingering your clitoris."

"I grab your ass, pushing your cock deeper inside me. I want it all!"

"The heat and wetness of your vagina wraps around my penis, enveloping it, bringing me to the verge of climax. I pump faster and harder, grinding against you, and my penis can't take any more. I cum inside you as you gasp, and we collapse into each others' arms, breathing each other's breath."

"I can feel your dick throbbing inside my hot pussy."

"Staying inside you, we hold each other, loving the closeness. Gradually, my penis relaxes, and I pull out of you, but still holding each other, we fall asleep in each other's arms, a loving and satisfied smile on our lips."

God, maybe I should have been a writer for Penthouse. I mean, it's not Shakespeare, but it got the job done.

"Nice, baby," Barbie said. "Was it good for you?"

"I think I need a cigarette!"

"You smoke, lover?"

"No, I don't, Barbie. It was just a figure of speech. Yes, it was very good."

Actually, it was. Not like the real thing, obviously, but still satisfying. It was exciting to be so sexual with this sensuous woman.

Especially when I was looking at Barbie's picture while we were interacting.

"So, tell me about yourself," she said.

Shouldn't we have gotten to know each other *before* we had virtual sex? Oh well.

"I'm an art director for an ad agency," I said. I figured the fewer lies to keep track of, the better. I already had to remember a different name and home town.

"Sounds interesting."

"Well yeah, it sounds like it, but sounds can be deceiving. I mean it's an okay job but I don't have as much creative outlet as I would like. And it doesn't help that my boss is an ignorant asshole."

"Oh, that's too bad," Barbie said. "I'm afraid that's a pretty common complaint, though. How is he an asshole?"

"Oh, Ed's a jerk. Thinks he's incredibly funny and clever when he's really just embarrassing. And he's a fucking lousy manager."

I realized after the fact that I had used Ed's name. Careful! At least I hadn't said his last name. And I have to be sure to not mention the name of the agency.

"I'm sorry honey."

"He gave me the chance to do some creative stuff," I continued, appreciating the opportunity to vent, "and I did some really good work on it. Then the bastard snatched it away from me."

"Hmm, that sucks."

"I know. Sometimes I think I should try to find a new job, one that's more challenging and rewarding. But I do get a decent salary. I don't think I'm going to find another job that would pay me as well."

"Well, good luck," Barbie replied. "I hope it gets better."

"Thanks."

"Gotta go. We'll talk later."

"Okay, Barbie. This was very nice. Thank you."

"Sure, lover. I'm rubbing my nipple for you."

And she was gone. I smiled at the sentence that had apparently become her sign-off line, the line that I had introduced in our first conversation.

I blew out a long sigh and sat back, shifting in my chair, rearranging myself in my pants again. There may not have been a lot of depth in my relationship with Barbie, but there did seem to be some length and girth!

I looked up at the Facebook menu bar again, and again, there were a couple of notifications, a new friend request, and another personal message.

From JuleighAnn Harper. Why was I suddenly feeling ashamed?

"Hi Gus. How are you tonight?"

"I'm doing very well, JuleighAnn. How are you?"

"I'm fine. We were talking last night, among other things, about photographs of my lake. I wanted to let you know that I uploaded some more a little while ago."

I pulled down the Notifications menu and saw that she had indeed.

"Thanks for letting me know," I replied. "I'll go check them out now."

I clicked on the link to the new pictures and was blown away.

The first one I saw was of a lake that was frozen over, dusted with a thin layer of snow. The lighting was bright and from a low angle, as if early in the morning. Standing on the ice, and looking toward the viewer, toward JuleighAnn, was a coyote, seemingly relaxed, curious but unafraid. As a caption to the picture, JuleighAnn had typed: "Adopt the pace of nature: her secret is patience. – Ralph Waldo Emerson."

The next one was muted, almost black and white, but not quite. And it was dark, as if a gloomy day was turning into an even gloomier evening. It looked frigid. Again, there was ice on the lake, but JuleighAnn had focused on a particularly dark gap in the trees on the opposite shore. The picture was lonely and foreboding. The caption said, "If you gaze long into an abyss, the abyss will gaze back into you. – Friedrich Nietzsche."

There were others too, and I lingered on them, thinking not only about the photographs, but about the photographer. The remarkable, mood-evoking images she could glean from a common and undistinguished setting astonished me.

Besides the artistry of the photographs, what really surprised me was the sudden feeling of guilt I felt. Here was a truly lovely person, not just physically beautiful, but with some real depth, a multi-dimensional person with no apparent guile or conceit.

And here I sat, a shadow figure with a counterfeit profile, hiding behind an anonymous photograph, and who had just engaged in verbal sexual intercourse with a woman I had never actually met.

What I thought was odd was the fact that I didn't feel guilty about it concerning Evelyn, the wife I had promised to be faithful to, to love and to cherish until death us do part.

I felt as if I had betrayed JuleighAnn.

"JuleighAnn," I typed, "those are beautiful! You're an amazing artist."

"Thank you, Gus. But I just shoot what I see."

"No, it's not just that. I'm an artist myself. I know it's more than a point and shoot situation. You see extraordinary things in the most ordinary settings. And you're able to capture them in your pictures."

"Gus, that's so nice of you to say. Thank you."

I went back and looked at some of her other photos, clicking 'Like' on several.

"Well," she continued when the message window popped up again, "I just wanted to let you know. Thanks again."

"I'm glad you did, JuleighAnn. Thank you."

"Good night."

I closed the message window and looked through the rest of the pictures. When I finished with her lake photos, I opened the album of her selfies. Once again, I marveled at her beauty, at how seeing her face made me want to be near her.

So did a lot of other people, men in particular. The pages were full of remarks from men commenting to her about her beauty. In looking through the various pages, I noticed that two or three were regulars, constantly giving compliments about 'her great beauty,' 'her kissable lips,' etc. In fact, whenever I came to one of her soft and beautiful self-portraits, I could count on seeing at least one of those men's names in the comments.

I certainly couldn't argue with their observations, and JuleighAnn was always gracious and thanked them. But it just seemed kind of sad to me.

The most prolific compulsive complimenter was an older married man who, on almost every face shot, made some kind of oozing remark like, "My dear JuleighAnn, your beauty warms my heart," or "So wonderful to wake up and see this lovely photo first thing," or "You have a gorgeous smile, JuleighAnn. I love these pictures!" His unceasing declarations of her beauty were usually littered with hearts, too.

Pitiful.

I determined that I would be more discreet than that. And indeed, when I offered a remark – well, often it *was* a compliment. I mean how could I *not*? But at least I tempered it with humor, or some form of deeper insight.

I found myself wanting to upload some of *my* photographs. I was a pretty good photographer myself. As I said earlier, I had taken a lot of photographs when I was in Boston a few years ago. My style was much different from JuleighAnn's. More bright, more colorful, less moody. But people often told me that I had a good eye.

Feeling a little ashamed of my carnal shenanigans a few minutes earlier, I determined to do something productive. I opened my 'Pictures' folder and began searching for the Boston photos I had taken.

But still, Barbie was there in the back of my mind.

Damn!

When Lanelle was thirteen years old, I took her on a hike in Chautauqua Park, on the southwestern edge of Boulder, near the Flatirons. It was a gorgeous day in late April, just after her birthday. The weather started out kind of chilly, but it was sunny and gradually warmed up a little as the day progressed. There weren't that many people out, so we had the trail pretty much to ourselves.

My little girl was turning into a very pretty young woman, and I tended to snarl at every hormone pumping teenage boy who put his slimy eyes on her. Since there weren't many out that day, the hike was fairly free of such disturbances.

We had hiked to the base of the first Flatiron and were taking a rest amid the pine forest. I had been doing pretty well for a forty-four year old desk jockey, but Lanelle was seemingly tireless. While I was panting and draining my water bottle, she was exploring the clearing where we had stopped. But after a few minutes, she joined me on the fallen tree trunk that I was sitting on.

"You okay?" she asked.

"Yeah, I'm fine," I said. By that time, I had regained my breath. "How do you like it out here?"

"It's beautiful, Dad. You know I always like coming here."

I smiled and nodded, as I looked around.

"Are you and Mom getting a divorce?"

My head spun back toward her and looked at her face. When my eyes met hers, she looked down, as if she was sorry she had asked.

"Why do you ask that?"

"I heard you guys arguing last night, down in the living room," she said quietly. She seemed almost embarrassed.

"I'm sorry, honey," I said. Now, I was the one who was embarrassed. "I didn't realize we were that loud."

"It wasn't that loud, but loud enough that I could hear it. Mom said she didn't want to see you again, and you said 'fine by me!' " She looked up at me then. "Are you leaving?"

"No, baby, I'm not." I scooted closer to her and put my arm around her. "Married people get on each other's nerves sometimes, and say things they don't mean. Mom's probably forgotten all about that by now."

I knew better than that, but Lanelle didn't need to.

"Honest?"

"Honest!" I kissed her forehead, and she put her arms around me and squeezed. "Mom and I are going through a tough time, but we'll be fine."

"How do you know?" she asked, but she stopped abruptly as if that wasn't the whole question she wanted to ask. A moment later, she asked, "How do you know if someone is right for you?"

"You're asking the man you just thought was divorcing your mom?" I asked. She looked up at me with her eyebrows raised. "Sorry," I said. "Really, though, I'm not sure I could tell you. It's something indefinable. One of those things that you know when you see it."

If you're lucky.

Then, what she was asking finally sank in.

"Why do you ask?"

She looked up at me with a more humble expression.

92

"Tony Warwick asked me out on a date."

Tony Warwick was the cute little boy in her school picture a few years back, and I – wait, Lanelle was barely thirteen years old and this little creep wanted to take her on a date? I could feel the snarl coming on, but I held it in check, because I saw the somewhat nervous expression on Lanelle's face.

"How do you feel about that?" was the best question I could think of. It was noncommittal and gave me time to think of an answer.

"I don't know. I like him, but I don't know if I like him that much. You know, like if he's the right one or not."

"Part of me likes the fact that you're thinking about it in that way," I said with a fatherly smile. "But the realistic part of me knows that you're only thirteen. You don't have to choose your life partner right away. There's plenty of time, honey. And that's what dating is for, to get to know people. To give yourself time to figure out if they might be the right one."

She nodded, pursing her lips, as she looked across the clearing, thinking about what I had just said.

"Does that help?" I asked.

"Yeah," she replied. Then she cast a sidelong glance at me. "You know, you're smarter than you look."

That's my girl.

I love Saturdays. Who doesn't? Well, I mean besides people who have to work on Saturday. But I don't, so I love them.

Even without the alarm, I always woke up much earlier than Evelyn. She could easily sleep till eleven o'clock, sometimes even later. That meant that I always had several hours to myself. Time to spend on some kind of creative endeavor or household project.

This Saturday morning, I was going to start building Augustine's Facebook profile in earnest. I just wish I had more pictures of Augustine himself. I did an online search for more photos of 'young handsome man' for pictures that looked similar enough to Augustine's face, but with no success. So many of the faces had distinctive features. I would have to just make do with the two.

Until I read a personal message that was waiting for me. Another woman that I had befriended two or three days ago, Sara Linden, had reached out.

"Got a thing for George Clooney, huh?" she said.

And suddenly it clicked! The thing that had bothered me about the pictures. One of them, anyway. The one that I was using as my profile picture.

It was a picture of George Clooney from years ago, when he was about Augustine's age. The face had looked familiar, but at the time, I just couldn't quite put my hippocampus on it.

I had already eliminated one of the three photos I had chosen as Augustine's pictures, when someone recognized it from the internet. Now I sat there, stupidly looking at George Clooney for a few moments. The remaining picture was a black and white head shot. I looked back and forth at them.

And I came up with a story.

"Hi Sara," I replied. "It's actually kind of an inside joke. Some of my friends think I look like George Clooney did a few years ago. I don't think I do, but from a certain angle, I can kind of see their point. One of them even started using this picture as my ID on his cell phone, and it stuck. It's just kind of been a joke between us ever since."

I wasn't sure how to feel about my ability to lie so easily. But it sounded plausible. I went to the picture on my profile page and wrote a similar caption, explaining the situation in case anybody else noticed.

Crisis averted.

The ping sounded and another personal message appeared.

"Hi Gus." It was Chaisang.

"Hello, Chaisang. How are you?"

"I fine my friend. And you?" I sighed and got ready for another mundane conversation. I feigned interest, asking questions about her life, and occasionally tossing out somewhat suggestive remarks. But she never picked up on them. I don't know if it was because English was not her first language, or if she just wasn't interested. Turns out I wasn't either.

I got through it, though, by working on my Boston photos at the same time. Eventually, with all the long pauses and short responses I made, I think Chaisang bored of it too.

For my photos, taking my cue from JuleighAnn, I called up an earlier talent, that of creative writing. I wasn't as well read as I would have liked to have been, so having ready quotations to post with my pictures wasn't that easy.

But I used to write poetry when I was younger.

Yeah, I know, right about now you're wondering how anybody could have *ever* thought I was a nerd.

Well, I don't care what you think. I used to be pretty good, and I thought I could score a few points with JuleighAnn by posting some original prose with my photographs.

To start with, I picked a photo of a pair of ancient head-stones in Copp's Hill Burying Ground, one of the many historical cemeteries in Boston. This one was on the north end, overlooking the Charles River. The headstones dating back to colonial times fascinated me, as did the skull and crossbones carved into the stones as was common then.

I still clearly remember when I took the picture. After a few centuries, the inscriptions on the two separate head-stones were all but worn off. I have no idea who the people were. But the two headstones were placed close together and linked by several vines of coppery ivy growing across both of them.

So I looked at the photo for a while, trying to evoke a mood, experimenting with the prose that began forming in my mind, until I had crafted what I thought was a fairly respectable caption for the photograph.

"Two hearts, marching in cadence, beating in tandem, linked by love during life, remain coupled in eternity, though they beat no longer. – Augustine Smith"

Not bad!

I repeated the process with a few other pictures, study-ing the composition, the mood, and laboriously pumping out a line or two of drivel that sounded vaguely poetic. In about an hour's time, I had gotten several done. I uploaded the photos, wrote the captions, and posted them on my page.

Augustine Smith, so much more than just a pretty face!

* * *

Around ten-thirty, I could hear the ominous sounds of Evelyn moving around her bedroom. First thing in the morning, she usually moved with all the grace of Godzilla taking a stroll through downtown Tokyo.

I knew my pleasant, relaxing Saturday morning was about to come to an end. She opened my door and poked her head in. I think I would faint from shock if she ever knocked.

"You're still working on that?" she asked, looking at the MaxiMed material from Melanie and Bob that I still had. It was strewn across my desk as camouflage. Interestingly, her voice was soft, not really accusing.

"Yeah, I'm coming up with some good stuff," I replied casually, minimizing the Facebook window on my computer. She couldn't see the screen from the door, and I knew it was unlikely she would come around to see it. She was never interested in my work, but just in case, I had one of the files I had created Thursday night showing on the monitor.

"You've been spending more time than usual in here. Why don't you ever talk to me anymore?"

You've got to be shitting me!

"I talk to you. I just don't have a lot to say."

"We never talk about anything important anymore. You don't tell me your feelings." She had an expression on her face as if I had hurt her. She had done this before. Not very often, though, and with varying results, so I didn't have enough reference to determine the best way to react.

"Actually, I have," I said, coaxing myself to be careful. "But it usually ends up with you yelling at me about them."

"I never yell at you about your feelings," she protested. "But you never validate mine."

That was one of her favorite complaints, that I don't validate her, her feelings, her opinions, her intelligence. And yes, she *did* yell at me about my feelings, but I knew better than to argue that point.

"I'm sorry," I sighed.

"I know," she asserted. "You're always sorry, but nothing ever changes!"

I'd heard that one before, too. I just kept quiet, hoping it would blow over.

"If you cared *anything* about me, you'd be more considerate of my feelings, instead of just blowing me off like you do!"

I just sat there, silent.

"And now you just sit there, not saying a word, wearing your socks upside down. You look ridiculous."

Huh? My feet were sticking out the back of my desk, toward her. I looked down at my socks.

"They're tube socks," I said. "There's no right or wrong way to wear them."

"'Hanes' is stitched into the top of the toe," she pointed out, in a tone that indicated that I was the stupidest creature ever to walk the planet. "The seam is on the bottom. Why would you want to walk around on the seam?"

"What the hell difference does it make which way I wear my damn socks?"

"I don't care how you wear your stupid socks," she snapped. "But again, you didn't bother to acknowledge *my* thoughts on the subject. Like I said, you never validate my intelligence!"

If your intelligence was valid, it would stand on its own without needing me to validate it.

I was thinking that, but I didn't say it.

Because I could already see and hear the anger rising. These times were the worst, when she worked herself up without my even saying anything. It didn't matter if I responded or not.

So I didn't. I just sat there quietly, not saying a word. I honestly don't even know what she said after that. I tuned her out, partially at least, paying just enough attention to know when I needed to respond to a direct question, to nod or shake my head.

She went on for maybe twenty minutes, letting me know what a terrible person I was. What made her stop was that she was hungry. It was already well after eleven o'clock, so evidently feeling the hunger pangs, Evelyn finally cast one last sneer at me, then banged the door closed. I heard her stomp down the stairs and start rattling things around in the kitchen.

I couldn't wait till she left for her time out with Maggie this evening.

By now, you're probably thinking that I'm an incredible weenie. And as far as Evelyn was concerned, I guess I'd have to agree with you. But I had learned over time that to avoid, or at least to minimize the effects of her temper, I had to just roll over and take it.

Unfortunately, though, it didn't always work. As I heard Evelyn clomping back up the stairs and toward my den just a few minutes later, I lamented that today was apparently one of those times.

"Don't you even care how you make me feel?" she asked the moment she opened the door. I sat back from the computer with a sigh, prepared for another episode.

"Of course I care, Evelyn," I said calmly and quietly, trying not to further provoke her. "I'm just not sure what it is I did that made you feel bad."

"Exactly what I said when I first came in here," she responded indignantly. "You never talk to me, and when you do, you don't trouble yourself to validate anything I say."

I didn't bother to point out that her supposition that I *never* talk to her was invalidated by her statement of the way I talk to her when I *do*.

"Okay, Evelyn," I sighed, "I'm sorry if I made you feel bad."

"*If* you made me feel bad?" she snapped. She shifted her weight to her other foot and put her hands on her hips, tilting her head as she looked at me. "You're giving yourself an out. *If* you made me feel bad. I'm telling you, you made me feel bad!"

"Then I'm sorry I made you feel bad!"

"Don't you understand that?" she asked condescendingly. "Saying 'if' in an apology invalidates the apology."

"I know, you've told me that. I'm sorry I forgot."

"See? You're always apologizing, but nothing ever changes!"

"You know what, Evelyn?" I said, growing *really* tired of this. "I don't know how you've managed to stay with me all these years."

"Oh, I see it's time to start your little pity party!" she snarled.

"Evelyn, knock it off!" Her sarcastic remarks pushed my buttons like you wouldn't believe. Whenever I struck back, that's always what did it.

"I'm just trying to help you to see how what you do affects other people," she said, assuming a very logical and helpful tone of voice.

"You know, you're right," I said, shutting down my computer, "I *don't* give a shit. Try educating someone else. I'm sick of this."

I stood up and walked past her.

"Where are you going?" she demanded.

"Out!" I shot over my shoulder.

See? I actually had some balls. I only took them out and used them once in a while. I snatched my jacket out of the closet on the way out, and I heard Evelyn pounding down the stairs. But I didn't wait to hear if she had any more to say. I mean I knew she did, I just didn't want to be here when she said it.

* * *

It was a nice day to be out anyway. Sunny, and warm for December. I drove to Chautauqua Park and found a spot where I could sit and look at the Flatirons, the enormous wedge-shaped slabs of rock jutting up diagonally out of the ground. Boulder's a really outdoorsy town, and a lot of other folks were taking advantage of the nice weather too. The park was full of people hiking, riding bikes, picnicking.

But I knew a nice area, a little off the beaten path, which was usually isolated. There was even a bench to sit on, but few people seemed to venture over there, so I had it to myself.

Once I settled down there, I breathed a sigh of relief. Something was going to have to change! I started thinking again that perhaps it was time to consider separating from Evelyn. She was a mess, and she was dragging me down with her.

But then, all the unknowns began creeping in. Evelyn, whenever presented with the thought of separating, never seemed to take me up on it. I knew we didn't love each other, so that's not what kept us together. Maybe it was the security of marriage. But her family was well-situated, and she would be taken care of until she could get herself set up.

Maybe, like me to an extent, it was just the whole comfort zone thing. It was the life we were accustomed to, and breaking out of that was scary.

But other times, it seemed more like she was just overly concerned about what friends and neighbors would think.

Honestly, I didn't have a clue why the two of us were still together.

A few minutes of thinking about Evelyn made my brain hurt. I shook my head, rubbed my eyes, and pulled out my cell phone. I needed a break. I had the Facebook app on my phone, but I hadn't used it to sign into my surreptitious account yet. I logged out, then logged back in as Augustine Smith.

A few notifications were awaiting me, and I looked at them, feeling relief wash over me, as if my latest fix was now coursing through my veins. I even breathed easier.

But my breath caught in my throat when I saw a personal message from Barbie.

"Hi lover. How's your Saturday going?"

"Very well!" I lied. I wasn't Arden Chase now. I was Augustine Smith. "I decided to head up the north shore and commune with the ocean at Marblehead. How about you?"

There was no immediate response, so I scrolled down my timeline, looking at the sexy pictures. Well, some of them. Some of the erotic writer ladies posted sexy pictures of muscular men, wearing little or no clothing, striking provocative poses. The kind of men who could make any *well-built* man feel inferior. Average men like myself – well let's just say I didn't spend much time on those pictures.

But within just a few minutes, I received a response from Barbie.

"Great," she responded to my question. "We're doing the same thing. I'm at the beach too." I remembered she was in Miami.

"Cool! You wearing a bikini?"

"Well, no. It's not that warm. Just enjoying the ocean."

"I sure enjoyed our time last night," I said, wanting to get past the small talk.

"I did too, lover! My nipples were hard for an hour after that!"

"Hmm," I said. "You and me both! Well, not my nipples."

For a moment, I marveled at how easily I could do sex talk with someone with whom I had no connection, neither physical nor emotional. But that was a concern for *only* a moment, until she responded again.

"Probably feels good to be away from the office, huh?"

"Oh, you know it!" Not the direction I was hoping the conversation would go, but one I could definitely relate to. "Very nice to be out of the drama!"

"Drama?"

"Oh, you know, there's always drama in the workplace. For instance, I told you about my asshole boss snatching that job away from me. That job could have helped me get a new position that's available. It's between me and this guy I work with."

"What's he like? Is he as good as you?"

"He's okay," I said.

What? I'm just being honest!

"I mean he hasn't won nearly as many awards as I have," I continued, "but he's a decent enough designer. Kind of a jerk sometimes, though."

"How do you mean?"

"Joe's the kind of person who might kick you when you were down, depending on the audience, and if he thought it would get a laugh."

"You don't like him?"

I paused. Strange, the response didn't come right away. I had to think about it.

"I don't know. Like I said, he's okay, but I just get tired of his insulting sense of humor sometimes."

"Hmm. I'm sorry, lover."

"Oh, it's okay Barbie. Everybody has to work with jerks and assholes. It's nice to have weekends when we don't have to think about them."

"I guess you're right. You don't have to think about work when you're fucking somebody hot, huh?"

Okay, that's more like it!

"Damn right, baby!"

"Are you alone?"

"Yeah, just enjoying the view. The trees and rocks."

"I thought you were at the ocean."

Shit! Be careful, idiot! I'm supposed to be at Marble-head, Massachusetts!

"Yes, but it's a rocky beach, and there are trees around." Marblehead *was* rocky, but there were no trees on the beach. Hopefully she wouldn't know that.

"Sounds pretty. So, you want to fuck some more?"

I felt that excited flutter again. I felt a little guilt, too, but I plowed over that. Can't let a little guilt get in the way of casual sex with a beautiful woman, even if it wasn't real.

"You know it!" I replied.

"Good," she said, "because it's a little chilly on this beach now that I've taken my blouse off."

"Well, I've taken my shirt off, too," I replied. "Let me see what I can do to warm you up."

And we were off again. Within just a couple of minutes, Barbie and I were naked and sweaty, panting and moaning, rubbing and screwing, from two thousand miles apart.

And I loved it! I knew there was no substance to it. It was just words between two strangers who knew almost nothing about each other. In fact, I later realized that she knew more about me than I knew about her.

Because I hadn't asked anything about her. I didn't care. I just wanted the excitement of meaningless, unattached sex. I didn't have the balls to go out and do it for real, apparently. So this seemed like a good, and safe, alternative.

I didn't *want* to know about her. I didn't care what she did for a living. I didn't care about her family or lack of one. I didn't care if she had a dog or a cat. I basically didn't give a shit about her, other than the fact that she was good looking and sexy.

And I thought *Joe* was a jerk?

* * *

By a little after four o'clock, the sun was getting low in the sky. The sun didn't officially set until a little bit later, but it was already starting to dip down behind the mountains, and in the shade, an evening chill was settling in. I hadn't had anything to eat since breakfast, and I was feeling pretty hungry.

But I didn't want to get home before Evelyn left at five. I didn't want to see the bitch tonight.

She had called me when I was in the park, but fortunately she hadn't interrupted me while I was engaged in keypad coitus with Barbie. I answered my phone when she called, just so I knew what to expect. There had been times in the past that she had been so angry at me that she canceled whatever plans she might have had. Fortunately that wasn't the case tonight. She was still mad at me, but she was still going out with Maggie.

I felt like some Mexican take-out, and I thought this would be the perfect time for it, since Evelyn didn't like Mexican food. I wasn't sure where a restaurant was, other than one of my favorites on the other side of town. The GPS in my dash wasn't helping much, though. I was getting an error message. That had been happening fairly frequently lately, and now it was preventing me from satisfying my Mexican jones! Great.

I felt my phone vibrate, probably telling me of more Facebook notifications. But before I even checked Facebook, I realized that the phone could be my salvation. I opened a GPS app and typed "Mexican food." That's more like it! Gotta love modern technology!

By the time I neared my house, the aroma of burritos and tamales permeating my car, it was fairly dark. But up ahead, I could just make out the shape of Evelyn's little Miata as she drove away.

The house was such a peaceful place when Evelyn wasn't there. I went to the liquor cabinet in the family room and got an Old Fashioned glass down from the shelf. I dropped a couple of ice cubes in it and splashed some J&B over them. The chilled Scotch left an agreeable burn as it ran down my throat, settling with a pleasant warmth in my stomach. I dribbled a little more into the glass and tossed it back.

Much better! That certainly took the edge off the day.

I got a beer out of the fridge and carried it, along with my Mexican food upstairs and into my den, settling myself comfortably behind my computer. Yeah, this was the life!

Shut up. I never said I was an exhilarating character.

* * *

Time had passed by almost unnoticed, and by ten-thirty, I was feeling the effects of the scotch, the Mexican food and two beers. But during that time, I had enjoyed a rather thrilling evening. I had engaged in yet another sex chat with Barbie in Florida, and had flirted extensively with a couple of other ladies in different parts of the country. Not bad for an old, unhappily married man in Colorado.

But I could barely keep my eyes open. I shut down my computer and went to bed.

Are German Shepherds good dogs?" Lanelle asked. We were at the Boulder County Animal Shelter, looking at a young German Shepherd, a few months old. She looked up at us through the wire door of her pen as we considered her for adoption. It was summertime, Lanelle was thirteen, and Evelyn had finally consented to letting her get a dog.

"All dogs can be good," I replied. "They just have to be trained."

"No, I mean are they good dogs, or do they shit in the house?"

"Lanelle," I said, trying not to smile, "what have I told you about that? We don't talk like that."

"Yes, you do, Dad. But what difference does it make? Shit, poop, doodie, they're all just different words for the same thing."

I turned and wiped my hand down my face, taking the opportunity to smile and get it out of my system.

"So, what about it, Dad?" she persisted. "Are German Shepherds good dogs or do they shit in the house?"

"Why are you asking this?" I wondered.

"Mom told me we better get a good dog. That she doesn't want one that shits in the house."

"I see." Thanks Evelyn. I sighed. "Well honey, like I said, it's just a matter of training. In fact, this puppy's old enough, she may already be housebroken."

Lanelle looked down at the pup, and the movement of her head caught the dog's eye. She turned and looked attentively at Lanelle, tilting her head slightly. Then as Lanelle smiled at her, the dog's face relaxed in the classic dog expression, its mouth open, tongue hanging out, looking every bit like a happy smile.

When Lanelle knelt down in front of the door, the dog stood up, its awkward tail swinging wildly back and forth. Lanelle put her hand out and the pup stuck its nose through the wire, sniffed and licked her fingers. Lanelle's heart was won over, and she stuck her hand through the door to pet the dog. The puppy, of course, loved that, and Lanelle's hand was soaked in no time.

"Dad," Lanelle said, looking up at me, her face beaming, "I love her!"

I was afraid of that. I took a deep breath as I thought this through.

"I'm not sure your mother would approve," I said, thinking aloud. "German Shepherds get pretty big."

"Well, that's perfect," Lanelle replied. "Nobody would bother me when I take her for a walk. Heidi will protect me."

"Heidi? You've already named her?"

"Yes," she said, turning back toward the dog. "Can we get her?"

"Well," I said hesitantly, "let's go check. They say puppies are the first to get adopted. Let's be sure she's still available."

Lanelle stood up, wiping her hand on her jeans. She cast another look at the puppy who was looking hurt, as if she couldn't believe we were actually leaving her. We started walking down the aisle toward the office.

Lanelle slipped her hand in mine. It felt a little warm and moist. I smiled and closed my hand over hers.

"I'm sorry I said shit, Dad."

110

I don't know when Evelyn had finally gotten home, but I knew from past experience that this would likely be one of the days she slept till almost noon. So I was able to spend even more time at my computer, engaging in my nefarious activities. I was hooked! And I had found several women who were more than willing to reel me in.

I purposely stayed away from women in Boston, to avoid any possible requests to meet in real life, and in so doing, had found a couple of women in Colorado who were open to extreme flirtation at least, if not outright sex talk. One lived in Durango, in the southwest corner of the state, the other actually lived in Denver.

Teri, the lady in Denver, was particularly enticing. She had bright red hair and was pretty damn uninhibited. She had tattoos on various parts of her body, which she was not afraid to show in photographs she uploaded to her profile. Celtic-looking markings down her arms, a coiled dragon across her back (what is it with tough chicks and dragon tattoos?), and a flower design across the back of her hips. She also had a fascinating intricately intertwined Celtic design that began at the front of her left shoulder, twisted around the side of her breast (her hand was covering her nipple), down her side, over her hip, then twined down her shapely thigh and finally terminated above her ankle.

Something about it . . . I don't know, I just thought it was pretty hot.

We had flirted a little last night, so I was particularly happy to see that she was online this morning. I opened up the message window, where our conversation from last night was still showing.

"Hi Teri," I wrote.

"Hey, Gus," she replied almost immediately. "Coming back for more, huh?"

"Absolutely. Didn't get enough of your sweet stuff last night."

"Mmmm. You're looking pretty sweet yourself." That made me smile. I had to remind myself that she was talking about the fake picture, not me. But it still felt good.

"Thanks," I said. "But I've seen more of you than you've seen of me, and you look pretty damn good, girl! Love that full length shot. That's one hot body you've got on you!"

"Glad you like it. But you're right, I haven't seen much of you. Maybe we should fix that."

Uh oh.

"What do you mean?"

"Show me more of you, babe! You have any tats?"

"No, I don't," I replied. "I'm baby white. Sorry."

"That's okay. Let's see your baby white skin."

As I sat there thinking about how to handle this, she followed that up with another message, or rather a photo. A shot of a tattoo I hadn't seen before on her photo page. Her skin was very light, like her remark to me about 'baby white skin.'

Full frontal, below the hips.

She was shaved or waxed. I didn't know which and frankly didn't care. And in place of pubic hair, there was a tattoo of a red heart, wrapped in strands of barbed wire.

Oh yeah, and her smooth pussy was plainly visible below it!

As you might imagine, it was rather distracting. But despite the distraction, it still gave me an idea. I could send her a similar photo, without showing my face and giving away my real identity. She had already shown me hers. It was time for me to show her mine.

Well, not my pussy but, oh you know what I mean.

Did I really want to do that? Hell yeah! Did I jump at the chance? Well, not quite. I crept up on it cautiously. I wasn't a news hound, but I had seen enough to know about Carlos Danger and the Weinergate scandal. Granted, I knew I wasn't a public figure, and there were probably plenty of nobodies like me sending pictures of their junk back and forth.

But still I was cautious.

Hiding behind Augustine, though, made me feel a little more brave. So finally, I worked my courage level up to almost manly. I listened for any sounds coming from Evelyn's room. Not hearing any, I stood up and dropped my drawers. After doing a little gentle stretching (a man should never engage in full-frontal nude photography without stretching first!), I snapped a picture with my phone.

I stared at the picture for a minute or two, deciding if I really wanted to go through with it. I knew I was no Dirk Diggler, but I decided it wasn't bad. Finally, I took a deep breath, clicked "Share" and sent it to Teri.

"Ooo, baby," she replied. "Nice poker!"

"Thanks," I typed with a smile, sighing as the adrenaline gradually dissipated. I pulled my pants up and settled back in my chair. Teri followed it up with a close up of her breasts, now no longer hidden by her hand. Both nipples were pierced, and a curved barbell hung down from each of them.

I cringed a bit as I thought about what it must have felt like, but at the same time, I was incredibly turned on.

"Nice!" I managed to type. "Did it hurt?"

"Of course," she said. Duh! "But isn't it sexy?"

"Very! I want to play with them with my tongue!"

"Mmmm! I'd like that!"

"Really?"

"Ooo, yeah. Put your lips against my nipple. Grab the barbell with your teeth and pull."

So she was into rough stuff. I was a neophyte at that, but I played along for a few minutes. But during those few minutes, we had virtually grabbed and pulled at each other, poked and prodded, even bitten.

But then Teri informed me that she had to get ready to go meet her boyfriend.

Her boyfriend?

"Really?" I asked nonchalantly. "Where are you going?"

"Axe is doing a Harley ride for charity." Her boyfriend's name is Axe? "Then we're going to lunch at the Greased Hawg Saloon."

"Hmm, too bad I'm so far away."

"I know," she replied. "Maybe we could slip into the restroom when Axe wasn't looking. Do some of this shit for real!"

Uh, ahem.

"Yeah, I'd love that!"

God, why did I have to live so damn far away? Boston was about two thousand miles away from Denver.

Of course, Boulder was only about thirty miles away.

* * *

Evelyn hauled her lazy ass out of bed at about eleven-thirty. Fortunately, though, I didn't have to see much of her. I was leaving by the time she came downstairs. I just said I had to go meet someone and didn't have time to elaborate.

I'd have to come up with something later on, but I didn't have to worry about it now.

I had looked up the Greased Hawg online. Wasn't a place I was familiar with, but I saw it was on west Colfax, one of the main streets that goes all the way through the Denver metro area. I knew I wouldn't exactly blend in, but I did have a black leather jacket. That and my aviator sunglasses, I thought, helped.

Don't ask me what I was hoping to accomplish. I knew Teri wouldn't know me from Adam.

Or Augustine.

I just wanted to see her. Instead of just looking at static photographs on Facebook, this was an opportunity to see her move and talk, interacting with other people.

And see if she went to the restroom with anybody when Axe wasn't looking.

Anyway, once I walked in the door, I felt self-conscious. I wasn't a biker. I had driven up in a BMW, parked it next to a row of Harleys and Hondas.

And gotten some piercing looks from a few pierced bikers out front.

Those inside, who hadn't seen me drive up, still seemed to know something was up with me. But I tried to ignore it. I pulled my sunglasses off in a smooth motion that I hoped channeled Marlon Brando or James Dean.

Or I would have even been happy with Fonzie.

There was no hostess at the entrance, so I looked around, as if I was searching for a table, but I was also looking for Teri. She wasn't here yet.

I saw two empty tables and, hooking my sunglasses in my shirt collar, I started walking toward one of them. I felt a lot of eyes on me as I walked through the tavern, but I tried to act unconcerned. One of the tables was in the corner, and that's the one I sat down at, facing the other one, hoping that Teri and Axe might take it when they arrive. I didn't have to wait long to find out.

As I looked at the simple menu on the table, an older, tough-looking woman with tan leather clothing and darker leather skin approached me. Her hair was a flat dark brown, with no variation in shade, no highlights or anything, except for the sharp line where the grey roots had grown out about a half inch. She didn't say anything, just nodded her head upward once, which I took to mean something to the effect of, 'Whaddaya want?'

"I'll start with whatever's on tap," I said. I didn't know if they had any microbrews, nor did I like the reaction I imagined if I ordered a Blue Moon, or perhaps a nice Hefeweizen. "And a cheeseburger and fries."

She silently turned and headed back to the bar, and as she did, the front door opened and a pretty redhead in tight blue jeans and a brown leather jacket came in. She was followed by a guy who looked as if he chewed razor blades rather than shaved with them. He looked to me like a creature from a nightmare.

But he *did* fit in very well here at the Greased Hawg.

Teri and Axe saw the table next to mine and made their way towards it, greeting friends on the way. As they got closer to the table, they both looked at me strangely. Teri looked away after a moment, but Axe held my gaze longer, narrowing his eyes a bit.

Until I looked away.

Shut up, you would have done the same thing.

Teri sat down in the chair closest to me, which meant that her back was to me. Unfortunately, that meant that Axe was facing me. Fortunately, Teri's body usually blocked him.

Teri took her jacket off and turned to hang it on the back of her chair, and when she did, our eyes met briefly. She smiled, but then, the moment now past, she turned back around.

She was wearing a tight tank top, and as her bright hair moved around, I could see the head of the dragon tattoo above the back of the neckline, dark against her white skin. The Celtic designs on both arms were visible, of course, and occasionally, if she lifted her left arm, I could see the top of the intricate design which I knew snaked down the length of her torso and leg.

Having seen her body online, I was having a hard time looking away, though I forced myself a few times when I noticed Axe looking at me. I was happy when 'Flo' came back with my cheeseburger. Now I had something else to concentrate on.

The burger was pretty good. A little greasy, but tasty. The beer wasn't anything special, but it wasn't bad. I was about three quarters of the way through my lunch when Teri stood up and headed toward the restroom. Now, in full view of Axe, I made it a point to not watch Teri walk away.

I finished my lunch and wiped my mouth on my napkin, and I was belatedly starting to question the wisdom of my coming here. What the hell did I hope to accomplish anyway? So I saw Teri move around a little. So what? I realized it was a stupid idea.

Then Teri reappeared, and I saw her walking toward me. Well, she was walking toward her table, but she was facing me, and I had a hard time looking away. Earlier, when I said her jeans were tight, that was like saying my beer was wet. Obvious and accurate, but not the whole story.

'Painted on' is, I think, an overused phrase, but in this case, I think it worked. Because I could see her shape, if you know what I mean.

I watched as she sashayed through the tavern, and I had the impression that other men were watching too. I say I had that impression, because I couldn't quite pull my eyes away from her to look at the men. She didn't seem to mind, though. In fact, as she approached, she saw *me* watching her, and she smiled at me again.

That is until Axe stood up, noisily pushing his chair back.

"What the bloody fuck are you looking at, asshole?" Need I say there was a bit of an edge to his voice?

"Nothing, sir," I said meekly. Okay, I wasn't *quite* that big a dork, but I might as well have been. I looked up at this side of beef standing over me, attempting to act as if nobody else there had my attention. But that was difficult, because now, Teri was beside him, just a few feet away from me. Despite Axe's size, Teri had a greater pull on my attention.

Like her tight, contour hugging jeans, her tank top was also tight. Her breasts pressed firmly against the fabric and, even though she was wearing a bra, it wasn't very thick. I could see the faint outline of her nipples, and of the barbells. I was still sitting down, and they were at eye level. So can you blame me for glancing there again? And that's all it was, just a glance, really. But that's what I saw in that glance.

At least that's what I saw until Axe punched me in the left eye. It felt like a cinderblock, but I'm pretty sure it was just his fist. What made it worse was that, when he punched me, my head was knocked against the wall behind me. And after I bounced off the wall, I ended up back in Axe's hands. He was pulling back for another sledgehammer blow when Teri held his arm.

"Axe," she said, "leave him alone. He didn't do any harm."

Her voice seemed unnervingly calm considering the ravages that Axe had just visited upon my head.

My left eye was already swelling, but through my right one, I could see Axe processing her words, and her hands on his arm. He didn't want to let it go, but it seemed as if Teri's will was stronger than his.

He reluctantly pushed me back into my chair, but at least he had the satisfaction of seeing my head bounce off the wall again. As they got their jackets from their chairs, they walked away. Teri never looked back, but she sure was attentive to Axe.

As if the whole episode had turned her on.

After they left, I could sense heads turning towards me, but I didn't bother to look up at them. I was too embarrassed. I *did* look up, though, when the waitress approached and, in a sweet gesture of care and concern, placed the check on my table. Without a word, she turned and went back behind the bar.

A real softie, that 'Flo.'

I fished a few bills out of my wallet and left them on the table, and I got up and staggered out the door.

When I got to my car, I stopped in my tracks, trying to focus. Looking at the driver's side, I saw a long, deep scratch etched down the length of the car from headlight to taillight. I looked around. A couple of bikers were watching me, leaning against the wall, with cold, inscrutable expressions on their faces. I quietly got in my car and pulled away.

After I left the Greased Hawg, it didn't take me long to realize that a second eye was a piece of equipment easily taken for granted when driving. It took me a few moments to get used to not having binocular vision, and the lack of depth perception was a little unnerving. I was keeping to the right lane, driving slowly. That gave me time to also consider the pain radiating out from the half a tennis ball that had risen up on the back of my head.

I drove back to Boulder. I didn't want to go home yet, but I didn't know where else to go. Home sounded comfortable, but it also included Evelyn. And now, besides needing a story for where I went, I also needed a story about how my face had been rearranged. I had never been in a bar fight before, and I admit there was a certain masculine appeal about that.

Don't try to distract me with the fact that I never threw a punch.

Some Sunday! I was almost looking forward to going back to work tomorrow.

* * *

I was almost home, having come up with no alternative. But when I came to a park a block away from my house, I pulled in, coming to a stop near an empty playground. I shut off the car and put my head back against the head rest, flinching at the pain in the back of my head.

I pulled myself out of the car, and the chilly air revived me a little. I made my way to a bench, sheltered from the breeze by some trees, and I sat down. I took several deep breaths, trying to relax, but I jumped when my phone rang.

It was Evelyn. Damn!

"Hello?" I said.

"What are you doing?" she asked.

"I had to meet somebody for work," I replied. I had to be careful, coming up with a story on the fly.

"On a Sunday?"

"Yeah, it was the only time they were available. We're starting on their account tomorrow, so I needed to get some information."

"What's wrong?" she asked.

"What do you mean?"

"You don't sound right. Your voice is shaking."

Shit. I'm not going to get a chance to think about a story.

"I was mugged," was the first thing out of my mouth.

"What? Where?"

"West Denver, on Colfax."

"You were robbed? Did he get your wallet?"

Good old Evelyn, always thinking about me.

"No," I replied. "I panicked and punched the guy, and he took off."

That actually sounded pretty good.

"You punched a mugger? Was he armed?"

"He had a knife. But he seemed scared."

"You punched an armed mugger? You could have been killed!"

"Well, I wasn't."

"Have you called the police?"

"No." That's all I needed! File a fraudulent crime report with the police. "He was wearing a mask, so I didn't really see the guy's face. And he didn't get anything from me, so I just don't want to bother."

There was a long pause.

"I'm okay, by the way," I finally said sarcastically. "I got punched myself, but I'll be fine."

"He hit you?"

She's quick like that. Can't pull anything over on *her!*

"Yeah, he punched me in the eye. Anyway listen, I need to go. I'll be home in a while."

I didn't wait for a response and I disconnected.

I was fairly happy with the story I had come up with, especially being on the spur of the moment. I thought it seemed believable, but there was also the heroic he-man quality to it that I liked. I hoped I could deflect any additional questioning, but I felt that I had a pretty good basis to build on, if necessary.

I started to put my phone away, but I noticed that there was a Facebook notification icon showing at the top. When I opened the Facebook app, I saw that there were actually several notifications. A friend request, a friend approval, and a couple of other posts from people I get notifications about.

One was Teri.

"A cager driving a BMW was at the Greased Hawg this afternoon when we were there. He was checking me out. That was kinda hot, but a big mistake! Axe pounded him, lol. Keyed his car on the way out, too. lmfao"

So I'm a 'cager'? What the hell is that?

I opened a browser on my phone and typed it in. The first link that appeared was to a web site called urbandictionary.com:

> cager
> a popular word among motorcyclists and bicyclists for four wheeled motor vehicle drivers. The term is often used in a derogative sense, because the car body effectively forms a cage, isolating the said driver from having to interact with other road users.
>
> The term was coined by motorcyclists.

Well, what the hell did I expect, driving a Beemer to a biker bar? I was an idiot.

But despite that belated realization, and the wisdom that should have come with it, my one good eye kept going back to what Teri said in her status update: "He was checking me out. That was kinda hot."

So that smoking hot redhead wasn't turned off by an old fart checking her out. I know, there was the part where she 'laughed out loud' about Axe pounding me, and where she 'laughed her fucking ass off' about him keying my car. But the part that held my attention was the fact that she thought it was hot that I was checking her out.

Me, not Augustine.

World class idiot!

And to prove it, the next thing I did was open the message window and select the conversation that Teri and I had engaged in.

"Hey Teri, I saw your post about the guy in the bar. Sucks to be him, huh?"

She responded almost immediately.

"Yeah. Axe is fuckin jealous. Kind of tiring, but kind of hot too."

I didn't want to talk about Axe, or how she thought his jealousy was hot.

"Good thing I can hide my tracks, huh?"

"You're fine babe. 2000 miles is pretty good protection."

Right, I'm in Boston. What would she think if she knew that I was just a few miles away? That I had been just a few *feet* away from her at lunch?

That I was the sorry bastard that Axe had pounded?

Well, all I can say is that at least I didn't further prove my idiocy by revealing that I was really the geezer who had been ogling her at the Greased Hawg.

* * *

It was approaching five o'clock and it was getting dark by the time I got home. I pulled into the garage very carefully, turning my head back and forth, watching both sides with my monocular vision.

Evelyn looked shocked when I walked in. I knew why. I had looked at myself in my rear view mirror, and I wasn't a pretty sight. My eye was a dark purple and was swollen almost shut. The discoloration faded to kind of a sickly olive color around the edges, and the amount of real estate the discoloration took up on my face was rather remarkable. The bump on the back of my head had gone down a bit, but was still pretty tender.

"Oh my god!" she said. "Sit down."

She went into the kitchen and came back a minute later with a plastic bag full of ice, wrapped in a towel. She put it against my eye, a little too hard, and I winced and pulled away.

"Well, I'm sorry!" she said in her huffy voice that didn't sound sorry at all. "I was just trying to help." She held the bag out to me.

"I know you were, Evelyn, and I appreciate it," I said, taking the ice from her. She scoffed at the last part. "It just hurt, that's all."

"Maybe you should go to the doctor."

"I'll be fine," I said in a consoling tone. "Besides, you hate doctors."

"They serve a purpose, in an emergency."

"Well, this isn't an emergency. It's just a black eye."

"Fine," she said, putting her hands up in surrender. "I obviously don't know anything."

"Oh my god," I said under my breath, closing my remaining eye and hoping that Evelyn wasn't about to take off on yet another tirade.

"I'm just concerned, that's all."

"I know, Evelyn," I said quietly and evenly. "I'm just not feeling well." I hoisted myself to my feet. "I need to go lie down."

"Okay, fine," she said with a tone of resignation.

Feeling more physically drained than I could ever remember, I dragged myself up the stairs and into my room. Collapsing onto my bed, I eased my head gently down on my pillow. I think I was asleep within a minute or so.

Heidi was indeed housebroken. A real plus in Evelyn's eyes. Evelyn still didn't like the idea, especially knowing how big Heidi would get. But Evelyn gradually acquiesced. She and Heidi eventually developed a shaky acceptance of each other.

As Heidi grew, however, she became possessive of Lanelle. I noticed that when Lanelle had friends over, Heidi was wary of them. Lanelle was always able to calm her and eventually, Heidi would warm up to her friends. But there was usually some tension at the beginning.

That was with Lanelle's female friends. Boyfriends were a different story.

Tony Warwick had been an off and on boyfriend of Lanelle's when there were school functions that called for one. But mostly, they were just friends. They paired up occasionally for school projects too, like a history report they were collaborating on.

On this late fall Saturday, Lanelle was on the floor of the living room, petting Heidi, while Evelyn and I were sitting there reading. I noticed Lanelle looking up and me, and I put my book down.

"Dad, I know you're a history buff and all," Lanelle said, "but this has to be our project."

"I understand," I said, my hands raised defensively in front of me. Although I admit I was kind of salivating over the topic, the *beginning of the American Revolution. I really loved New England history.*

But I knew they were more than up for the challenge. They were both excellent students. And Lanelle was developing into quite an artist, which of course made the Art Director in the family very proud. And she was planning some exquisite art panels to go with the project. "I promise I'll keep my nose out of it," I said.

That was when the doorbell rang and Lanelle got up to open it. As expected, it was Tony, and he came in to the entry, all smiles and good looks as always.

"Hi, Mr. and Mrs. Chase," he said when he saw us. Nice, polite kid.

I noticed that Heidi was alert, though, keeping her eyes on Tony, every muscle tense and ready. She was a little over a year old now, and easily seventy pounds. Evelyn was saying something to me, but I wasn't listening. I got up and walked toward the entry.

When Tony reached out and touched Lanelle's arm, Heidi lunged for him. Fortunately I had just grabbed her collar. Tony jumped back, his face as white as the whites of his eyes, which were now much larger than usual.

Heidi was barking and snarling, and as I was only vaguely aware of Evelyn shouting in a panic behind me, it was all I could do to hold Heidi back. Lanelle, distracted at first by Tony's fear, turned her attention to Heidi. She put her hand up in front of the dog's face and firmly said, "Heidi, down!"

That seemed to short-circuit the dog's anger, though she was still tense, keeping her eyes keenly focused on Tony.

"Come on," Lanelle said to Tony, directing him to the stairs. Heidi's eyes followed them, and she pressed toward Tony. It was all I could do to hold her back. As Lanelle and Tony headed up to

her room where they were going to work on the project, I dragged Heidi toward the back door. She liked going outside, so the open door seemed to flip a switch.

I closed the door and went back to the living room, where Evelyn was seemingly in a mild state of shock.

"Something has to be done about that animal," she said, one hand pressed to her chest.

It was the middle of the night, but light from the full moon flooded through the window. I felt a movement in the bed next to me, a rustling of the sheets, and Teri's hand was on my chest. She snuggled up close to me and we kissed, and as we did, I felt her hand move down.

When it reached an obstruction, she took it firmly in hand.

She put a leg over mine and began rubbing her pussy against it, and I could feel changes taking place in my favorite part of me. Teri did too, and she sat up and got on top of me, straddling me. She slipped my now erect penis inside her as the moonlight sparkled on the stainless steel barbells through her nipples.

She put her hands on my knees and leaned back as she continued the up and down motion. I looked down at her smooth pussy, and in the shadows, I could just make out the barbed wire wrapped heart tattoo.

I reached up and took the barbells between my fingers and pulled. Teri followed them, leaning forward, and she supported herself on her hands against my headboard. I raised my head and put my mouth around a nipple, sucking and biting, hearing the click of the metal against my teeth.

As she continued riding me, I lost the barbell. It was suddenly a bare nipple in my mouth, and I looked up into the face of JuleighAnn Harper, her dark hair billowing down around her face. Panting, she smiled at me and leaned back.

Okay, now I'm not going to try to make you think that this was really happening. Obviously it was a dream. But hot damn, what a dream!

JuleighAnn rode me for a while as I watched her sliding up and down, her breasts jiggling with the exertion. I could feel my hands on her hips, and I moved them up her sides and finally cupped her breasts with them. They felt great! Firm, but with baby soft skin. Except for her nipples. They were hard as I rubbed my thumbs across them a few times, still wet from my saliva, and I smiled as a moan escaped her lips.

I raised my head and looked down between her legs, where her lovely lady parts were slipping up and down on my corresponding man part, her thighs flexing and relaxing. JuleighAnn closed her eyes and put her head back, her dark hair bouncing around her shoulders. I lay there entranced, watching this beautiful creature make love to me.

As I watched, her face changed again. In fact, everything changed. Her slim figure got a little thicker, a little heavier. Her breasts sagged a bit, bouncing kind of comically. Her hair became shorter and lighter, and a little disheveled. She slapped up and down on me with less grace and more weight. Under my hands, I could feel the skin rippled with cellulite and stretch marks.

I watched with horror as JuleighAnn's face morphed into Evelyn's.

And it was at that moment that *I* finally realized it was a dream. Not because of the science fiction shape-shifting imagery that happened before that. Apparently my mind accepted that with no problem. Rather, I knew it was a dream because the shape she shifted into was Evelyn.

I knew that Evelyn wouldn't be making love to me in real life.

The horror of it was enough to wake me up and I found myself alone in my bed. The room was lighter than I expected, lighter than it was in my dream anyway. The back of my head and my eye were throbbing, but I could see in three dimensions again. Apparently the swelling was going down.

I sat up on the edge of my bed, adjusting myself uncomfortably as I did so. *That* swelling hadn't gone down yet. According to the clock, it was 5:45, fifteen minutes before my alarm. I reached over and turned the alarm off, then struggled to my feet.

It was going to be a long day.

* * *

As you might imagine, I got a lot of curious looks and questions once I got to work. I had a pretty impressive black eye. The swelling was gone by now, but the purplish black color could be seen from across the office.

After briefly telling my made-up mugging story at least four times, I finally made it to the safety of my office, closing the door and collapsing in my chair. I managed to focus on my work for a while, despite interruptions as others wanted to know about my mugging. After a few hours, I was happy with what I had accomplished, and I was glad that Ed had seen me come in, and had also seen the volume that I had gotten done. I was certain that my dedication would serve me well when it came time to award the new Senior Art Director job.

My self-congratulations ended when my cell phone rang. It was Evelyn.

Shit.

"There's a guy on a motorcycle who keeps riding by," she said. Her voice had a fearful quality to it.

"Really?" People on motorcycles were not that unusual.

"He's gone by several times. He keeps looking up at our house."

"What does he look like?" I asked, with a chill beginning to form around my heart.

"What difference does that make?" Evelyn asked angrily. "He looks like a big guy with a lot of hair. He looks tough and mean."

"Is he being threatening in any way?"

"No, he hasn't stopped, but he slows down every time he goes by our house and stares at it. I'm scared."

"Have you called the police?"

"No. Do you think I need to?"

"Well, I don't know," I said. "I'm not there. What do *you* think?"

"Can you come home?" There was a momentary tone of fear in her voice. Not something she reveals very often.

"Evelyn, what do you expect me to do? At best, it'll take me forty-five minutes to get home, and most likely longer than that. If he stops and tries to do anything, I'm sure he'll be long gone by the time I'm able to get home. And if the guy *is* there to cause trouble, what could I do against a violent, aggressive biker?"

"You think he's violent?"

"Again," I sighed, "I'm not there. I don't know. But if he is, the Boulder police are in a much better position to help than I am."

"Thanks, Arden," she said. Apparently she wasn't too scared to assume her sarcastic and demeaning edge, because the fearful sound was now gone from her voice. "I really appreciate your concern!"

"What the hell am I supposed to do from here?"

"You're just demonstrating once again that you don't feel anything for me!"

"Uh, Evelyn, I hate to break it to you, but that's not really a news flash. We haven't felt anything for each other for quite a while now."

"I hate you," she hissed, and she hung up on me. I sighed and put my phone back in the holder on my belt. I shook my head and closed my eyes, feeling the throbbing in my head returning.

Axe, if that *is* you, help me out, will ya?

* * *

I thought about it a little bit after that, but only in the back of my mind. I mean, of course it wasn't Axe. How could he have followed me from west Denver to my home in Boulder without me noticing? I hadn't even gone straight home. I spent some time in that empty and quiet park, resting and nursing my wounds and my pride. I would have noticed a motorcycle nearby. In fact, having been bashed by a biker just a short time before, my eyes and ears would have been particularly tuned for the sound of a motorcycle.

But I knew what Evelyn was like. I knew that she would often get herself worked up about something, be in a state of turmoil about it for hours, then take it out on me.

So I knew what to expect when I got home.

I tried to bury my mind in my work, which lasted only until Joe Polaski barged into my office.

"Trying to cheat me out of that job?" he asked. I turned around in my chair and looked at him. I'm certain my face reflected the confusion I was feeling.

"What the hell are you talking about?" I asked.

"I heard about you doing those MaxiMed comps and giving them to Ed." Joe's face was a rather awesome shade of crimson. "You're not even overseeing that account! I am!"

"Alright, cool your jets, Joe," I said, holding my hands up in front of me in a placating gesture. "That's not the way it happened."

"I don't care how it happened. It shouldn't have happened at all! I've never gone behind your back to take your jobs, or to influence a promotion decision."

"I didn't do that, Joe," and I stood up to face him. Apparently that was the wrong thing to do. Joe took it as a threatening posture and backed up.

"Listen," I said in a calm and quiet voice, "Ed came to me and asked – "

"I don't want to hear your fucking excuses!"

"Joe, come on," I said, trying to appeal to him. I'd never seen him like this, and I certainly had never been on the receiving end. "We're friends."

"No, we're not. I think you're a shitty friend, and you suck as a designer."

And he turned and left my office, pulling the door closed behind him with a little more volume than I thought was necessary.

I remembered the remark I had made to Barbie, the blonde in Florida, about office drama, and I shook my head at this case in point. It wasn't enough that I had the soul-curdling productions to sit through at home. I had to endure them at work as well.

Oh God, how I love Mondays!

* * *

It was an ominous drive home. I had called Evelyn later on, to find out how everything was going. She had been cold and noncommittal. She hadn't called the police, and nothing had happened.

FEAR. That was an acronym that Evelyn often liked to quote to me if I was worried about something. It stood for False Expectations Appearing Real. Yet Evelyn was the one who usually worried about something that did not come to pass. She was an expert in fear and worry, an expert who did not apply her own counsel.

But the coldness in her voice was the ominous part. Whenever I heard that, I never knew quite what to expect. It could be a blow-out that could go on for hours, or an icy silence. A cold shouldered brush-off where I would be ignored, but could retreat to my den in relative peace.

Needless to say, I was hoping for the icy silence.

It turned out better than I had hoped. Well, it's always better when I see Cyndi on my way past her house. She saw me and waved, and I waved back, knowing that, if Evelyn saw me, I'd have to explain again. But as I opened the garage door and pulled in, I saw that Evelyn's car was gone. I knew better than to feel *too* hopeful. Evelyn being gone just postponed the inevitable.

But still, it was good for now.

I went inside and saw a note on the kitchen counter.

> Decided to go out with some friends to-night. I'll probably be out late. No need to wait up.

I almost did a happy dance!

I don't know what friends she went out with, and I don't know where they went. I don't know why she would even think I *might* wait up for her. But I didn't care. It meant that I had the whole evening to myself.

And I didn't even mind that I had to fend for myself dinner wise. After the scene with Joe at work, and the fact that I was still smarting from having the MaxiMed design job taken from me, this was a welcome reprieve.

I didn't want to bother with dinner, so I ordered a pizza. While I was waiting for it to be delivered, I fired up my computer and logged into Facebook.

There were the usual notifications, friend requests and friend acceptances, but the one that caught my eye was a personal message from Barbie.

"Hey, lover. How was your day?"

"How much time ya got?" I replied when I saw she was online. I figured I could use a little time with her. Maybe even fit in some sex talk. That would really hit the spot right about now.

"All you need, babe. What's up?"

"Oh, it's just work. And I don't want to burden you with it. Just had a rough day at the asshole factory."

"It's no problem. If you want to talk about it, I'm here. And who knows? I might even be able to do something to help you relax."

It's like she read my mind.

"It was just the guy at work. I told you about him. Mediocre designer, insulting bastard. We had a blowup today, about the OTHER bastard I told you about, my boss. The job he gave me to do was one that my co-worker was overseeing. But my boss didn't tell him he was giving it to me. Well today, he found out about it, and thought I was trying to take it away from him, or earn brownie points toward the new position. Anyway, he was just a jerk, and didn't want to hear what really happened."

"Aw, I'm sorry honey."

"It's okay. I just feel like they used the sphincter stretcher on me."

It was then that I heard the doorbell and knew that my pizza had arrived. After paying the zit-faced kid, I put a couple slices on a plate, grabbed a bottle of beer and went back upstairs. In that time, though, apparently Barbie had grown impatient and left. She wasn't online any longer. And she hadn't even rubbed her nipple for me.

Great. Now I could add sexual frustration to my day.

Didn't last for long, though, as I saw that Teri was online. I sent her a greeting, and I took a couple of bites of pizza and a swig of beer while I waited.

"Hi Gus," she finally replied. "Sorry, can't talk. I'm with Axe."

Strike two.

I sighed and scrolled down my timeline, browsing anything that interested me.

And no, I wasn't pouting.

But it did kind of suck that I had the evening to myself and nobody to spend it with, even virtually. Then I remembered that there were some notifications that I hadn't checked yet. I looked at them and saw that one was a "Poke" from JuleighAnn.

Now I never understood the point of a Facebook poke. It seemed to me like a "hello," but without all the commitment, a greeting for people who don't want to go to the trouble of actually connecting with another person.

But this one was from JuleighAnn. I poked back.

"Hi Gus," I saw as a personal message appeared a few moments later, and I felt that weird fluttery feeling again when I saw it was from JuleighAnn.

"Hey, JuleighAnn," I typed. "You must have known I was missing you!"

I didn't know if that was coming on too strong or not, but it was too late now.

"Really?" she replied. She followed that with a smile face. That was encouraging. I didn't use those very much myself, but I could see now how they helped the receiver understand your meaning.

"Yeah, I'm just sitting here at home, feeling lonely, feeling sorry for myself."

"Oh, so anybody would do. I just happened to be the one to poke you, right?" As I was thinking about Barbie and about Teri, I actually felt embarrassed. But JuleighAnn quickly followed her remark with another smiley.

Phew!

"No," I said. "I've enjoyed our chats. I'm glad you poked me."

"So why are you feeling sorry for yourself?" she asked.

"Oh, it's nothing important," I said. "Just a bad day at work."

Strange how with JuleighAnn, it was just a bad day at work. I didn't have the urge to use that as an excuse or a segue into an episode of sex with her. That's not to say that I wouldn't love getting hot and freaky with her. But that wasn't the primary focus of my interest in her.

With JuleighAnn, I actually felt giddy. Let me emphasize here that I've never used that word in relation to myself. I'm just not a giddy person. But JuleighAnn sure seemed to be able to get my giddy up.

"I'm sorry," she replied. "I'm glad it's over."

"Yes, I am too. Especially now."

"Oh? Why now?"

"Because I'm chatting with you now."

"Oh, Gus, how sweet."

I'm sweet? Not many people have told me that!

I took a deep breath and let it out. I was impulsively about to take a few paces out on a limb.

"JuleighAnn," I typed, "I know we haven't known each other very long, but I feel a real connection with you, a real kinship."

There was a pause, and I watched impatiently, waiting to see her response. It finally came.

"Really?" was all she said. One word and a question mark. Obviously, I knew what the word meant, but I had no idea what *she* meant by it. I waited a bit longer, but nothing else came.

"I understand if that makes you feel uncomfortable or suspicious," I went on, "and I apologize if it does, but I assure you, I'm not trying to take advantage of you or anything like that. I just really like you."

"Well, it's not like there's very much you could do to me from two thousand miles away in Boston," she replied.

Was that a twinge of guilt I felt in response to that? I was being honest with her about my feelings, but not about who I was, or *where* I was.

"But the truth is," she continued, "I like you too, Gus."

And at that moment, I think I could hear angels singing.

"Well, what's not to like?" I typed. Then, after I sent the message, I cringed a little. Why did I always have to hide behind my sarcastic humor?

"I really like your sense of humor," she replied with yet another smiley.

"You know," I said, "I think I may have to marry you."

"Well, given our distance, maybe an online cohabitation might be in order, first."

God, I loved that girl!

We chatted for over three hours. During that time, both Teri and Barbie attempted contact but, uncharacteristically, I blew them both off. I only wanted to be with JuleighAnn.

"I see on your profile page," I said, "that you're a counselor. What do you actually do?"

"I work through three different local hospitals, on a consultant basis, to help patients and families deal with loss and grief."

"Sounds heavy," I said.

"It can be at times. I was inspired years ago by someone who helped my mother and me a great deal during her time in the hospital. As you can imagine, that was a rough time for both of us, and there was a counselor who had a very calming effect on us. She encouraged and assisted Mom in getting her affairs in order, and she helped me to come to terms with going on alone after Mom died.

"Well that was such a huge help to me that I wanted to, I guess you could say, pay it forward. I got some additional schooling and acquired my master's degree, and now I meet with terminal patients and their families, as a grief and end of life counselor. Obviously that's a very sad time for them, but it's rewarding to know that I've helped them to cope with a difficult situation."

Not just a pretty face!

"But what about you?" she asked. "You haven't told me much about your life."

"Not that much to tell, really," I said, as that little feeling of guilt returned. "I'm an art director in an ad agency. I've won a few awards, but I'm kind of burnt out on it. Except that I have an opportunity now for a new position, which I'm really hoping for."

As with Barbie, I decided it was easiest to be truthful about as many details of my life as possible, rather than trying to keep track of a lot of made up details. But to keep her from digging too much for more, I decided to change the subject.

"I noticed you changed your profile picture." It was one with Molson, her Golden Retriever, and JuleighAnn had the most adorable smile on her face. "I love it. It's a beautiful picture!"

That did take us in a different direction.

But I knew it wasn't a permanent solution.

Whenever we knew that somebody was coming over, we started putting Heidi outside ahead of time. That was a temporary fix of the problem.

But I also arranged for some professional training for her. She didn't take to it very well. When forced, she was reluctantly obedient, but still behaved aggressively, particularly toward men.

We were always happy about the fact that we rescued her. But not knowing her previous history, well that was really the only drawback to adopting a pound puppy. We began to wonder what she went through in her first few months to make her so distrustful and aggressive toward men.

I was the only exception. Gentle and playful, she was a perpetual puppy when I was alone with her, or even if Lanelle was with me.

Months went by and we just got in the habit of putting her outside before somebody came in.

In the spring, when Lanelle was fourteen, she and I decided to venture out for a walk. It was a beautiful day and we didn't want to stay inside. Heidi loved it too. Lanelle kept a tight grip on the leash, but Heidi often pulled away toward a tree or sign post, carefully sniffing every possible angle until Lanelle was able to pull her away.

"Can you take the leash?" she asked. "My arm's getting tired."

"Sure," I replied as I took control of the beast.

"Why do they do that?" Lanelle asked with a certain mystified irritation, as she worked the ache from her arm. "Dogs always have to smell where others have peed."

"They have to see who else has been here," I said, "leaving their little messages behind. She's just checking her pee-mail."

Lanelle looked up at me with that universal teen-age expression that goes with wondering why adults are so weird.

"Dad, really?" she said with that universal teen-age tone of voice. I smiled and shook my head.

"I think it's just a territorial thing," I said with a tone that indicated that I surrendered to her stronger will. "Animals leave their scent, marking their territory, and other animals smell it. Then they either respect it or challenge it."

"That's gross."

"On the other hand, maybe it's just sort of a 'Kilroy was here'."

"Who?"

"Never mind."

We walked for a while, enjoying the nice, spring weather. As we approached our long driveway, lined with aspen trees now clothed in yellow green heart-shaped leaves, Lanelle took the leash back so I could fish my keys out of my pocket.

"Why is the mailman up at the house?" Lanelle asked, and I looked up. A mail truck was parked by the front door. Usually the mail was put in our box at the street.

"I'm expecting some books I bought online," I said. "They should be getting here about now. Maybe that's it."

Evelyn had just taken a package from the mail carrier and he turned around. At sight of him, Heidi took off towards him, pulling the leash out of Lanelle's hands and knocking her off her feet.

It happened so quickly, the man didn't see what was coming. He tried to fend her off, but Heidi had fastened herself to his left arm. The man was yelling and fumbling with something on his belt.

In the seconds before I got there, I saw Evelyn trying to pull Heidi off the man. Heidi snapped at her, nipping her hand, and in that moment, the mailman fell backwards. He got the little canister off of his belt with his right hand and aimed it, just as Heidi turned back to him, now grabbing that wrist.

Sending a burst of pepper spray into Evelyn's face.

Evelyn was screaming, her hands over her face, the mailman was bellowing a continuous stream of curse words, and Heidi was barking and snarling, as I was finally able to pull her off of him. Lanelle came up on the porch, her knees bloodied from the flagstone and got Heidi calmed down, and together, we took her around to the back yard.

The mailman had gone by the time I got back.

I woke up Tuesday morning with my face aching a little. It was getting better, though, the color fading to a kind of splotchy olive/gold. I took some Ibuprofen for the ache and got ready for work.

Besides the ache in my face, I woke up with an inner turmoil. My long chat with JuleighAnn the night before, while wonderful, left me with that nagging feeling of guilt at my dishonesty. What a sap! I purposely created the fake identity for the sole purpose of being dishonest, with one goal in mind – chatting up beautiful women. Yet now that I discovered one I really liked, I found myself not wanting to continue the dishonesty.

Shaking my head at my own inconsistency, I finished getting dressed and left my room. I could hear Evelyn snoring in her room as I went past. I walked quietly as always, not wanting to wake her.

I sure didn't feel like dealing with her.

I don't know what time she got home last night. I was already asleep. I never tried to puzzle out where she went or with whom. I honestly didn't care, as long as she left me alone.

But my curiosity was aroused when I saw her purse on the hall table where she always left it. It had tipped over, and I saw a little spring-lidded felt-covered box peeking out of it. The kind of box you get from a jewelry store to hold a bracelet.

I picked it up and opened it. It was empty. But along with the box was a little card, also the kind you might get from a jewelry store, to go with a gift.

"Your legs must be tired," it said, "because you're constantly running through my mind!" It was signed by someone named Tom.

My thoughts, admittedly, were kind of mixed up. They ranged from, "What the hell's wrong with Tom?" to "The bitch is cheating on me!" Then, as Teri and Barbie and Jolene flashed through my mind, I had the self-deprecating thought that, "At least Evelyn had the courage to do it for real."

I don't know if that's really courageous or not, but coming on the heels of my feelings of guilt about my dishonesty to JuleighAnn, it didn't feel very comfortable.

I started putting the stuff back in her purse, and as I did, I saw a business card. I wouldn't have thought anything about it, except that I had never known Evelyn to collect business cards. The name on it was certainly familiar. Tom

Bratter. He was a Denver businessman. Rich and relatively good looking.

He had been in the news about a year ago, having been charged with the murder of his wife. It was a high profile case, and John Parsons, Evelyn's father, had defended him. It was his last case before he retired.

The evidence against Bratter was almost overwhelming, and during the course of the trial, there were numerous comparisons to the O.J. Simpson case. Especially was that so when Bratter was found not guilty. There were accusations of falsifying evidence and jury tampering, but nothing ever stuck.

Due to all the negative press, Evelyn's father had actually considered taking on at least one more case, just so that he wouldn't be retiring on such a controversial note. The man was influential in his social circles and was concerned that it might reflect badly on his own reputation.

In the end, he followed through with his plans, counting on the fickle nature of the media and on the short memory of the public.

The fact that Tom Bratter was Evelyn's illicit squeeze could certainly cast a shadow on John Parsons.

I stuffed everything back in her purse and left, resisting the urge to wake Evelyn and question her about the gift and the card.

My mental turmoil continued as I drove to work. By the time I got to my desk, coffee in hand, I had resolved what I was going to do. Well, about JuleighAnn anyway. I went into Facebook and logged in as Augustine, and before I even checked my notifications, I opened the message window and started writing.

JuleighAnn, I have something very difficult to tell you, and I honestly don't know how you're going to take it. My hope is that you'll read it all and understand, but I won't blame you if you're angry with me.

In the short time we've known each other, and the long chats we've had, I've come to like and respect you more than anybody I know. So I've decided that I can't continue being dishonest with you.

I'm not Augustine Smith. My name is Arden Chase, and I live in Boulder. I created a fake identity, frankly because I am extremely unhappy with my real life. I thought that navigating through Facebook, meeting beautiful women outside the constraints of my real life, would be exciting. And I was right. It was exciting, though in the end, pretty empty.

But I didn't expect to meet someone like you. Someone whose strength and integrity have ultimately made me feel ashamed at my own deceit. And it's because of you, JuleighAnn, that I now want to come clean.

About everything. Including the fact that I'm married. That point is the biggest contributing factor in my unhappy life, and I think that I've just about reached my limit in that department.

I hope you're still reading and are sympathetic to my reasons for this fallacy, but as I said, I understand if you are angry and want nothing more to do with me. All the details of my life I told you about are true except for the name, location and marital status. And my age. I'm 49.

I will send you a friend request from my real profile.

I look forward to hearing from you.

I took a deep breath and clicked the Reply button. I looked to the column on the right and didn't see her profile icon. She was not online. Probably at one of her counseling locations.

That difficult business done, I logged out and then logged back in as Arden. I found JuleighAnn's profile page and sent her a friend request. There were a number of notifications, but I wasn't interested. I closed Facebook and got to work.

* * *

The day was busy, which was good. That's not to say that my conflicting thoughts about Evelyn and JuleighAnn weren't distracting. But being busy at least made the day pass more quickly. I went into Facebook whenever I had a chance, but there was never a response from JuleighAnn.

Although I did notice that she had *seen* my message during the noon hour.

There was still no response by the end of the day, and with a heavy heart, I headed toward home. Traffic was unusually light, especially with Christmas approaching. Maybe a lot of people were already gone for the holiday, or maybe they were concentrated around the shopping centers. At any rate, my drive home was better than usual.

It was dark and I was still about ten minutes away when my cell phone rang. I could see on the illuminated face that it was Evelyn.

Heavy sigh.

"He's back!" she said with panic in her voice.

"Who's back?" I asked.

"The guy on the motorcycle. It's the same guy as yesterday. He's out front, and he stopped this time! He's looking up here!"

"Evelyn, hang up and call 911."

I disconnected and accelerated, weaving through the traffic which had gotten heavier now that I was in Boulder. It took me less than five minutes to get the rest of the way home.

The first thing I saw was Axe dragging Evelyn out the front door. The porch light was on and the door jamb was splintered. Evelyn still had her phone in her hand and was screaming into it. Axe punched her in the face, and I winced, remembering the force of the punch I received just the day before yesterday. That punch seemed to knock her out, the phone clattering from her hand, and as I sped up the driveway, my headlights casting harsh shadows against the house, Axe turned and looked.

He dropped Evelyn on the flagstone walk, and I registered that her head bounced on the stone. Then she was still. As I hit the brakes a few feet away from him, he seemed to recognize my BMW, especially the long key scratch in the paint. But the recognition was complete when I got out of the car.

"You!" he said.

"Yeah, me. Leave her alone, Axe." I was surprised at the forceful tone I was able to muster in my voice. "What are you doing here?" I was hoping to engage him in a verbal exchange long enough for the police to arrive.

"You been fuckin' around with Teri!" he said.

"What are you talking about? I've never met Teri."

"I saw all the shit you two were sending each other on Facebook. I saw her phone."

"What makes you think that was me?"

"I saw the location, dipshit. Pointed me right here."

With a sudden but admittedly late flash of brilliance, I remembered turning on the location feature on my phone the other evening when I needed to use the GPS app. I had forgotten to turn it back off. I remembered that that feature will display your location on Facebook. Complete with a map.

Idiot!

He was advancing toward me as we spoke, and despite the fearless tone of voice I affected, I was backing up. Unfortunately I wasn't far enough away when he rushed me and grabbed me by the throat. I tried to push him away, but his arms felt like steel cords.

His fingers tightened and I panicked when I couldn't draw in a breath. I was struggling, holding on to each of his wrists.

A fragment of self-defense instruction made its way into my waning consciousness, and I quickly lifted my knee, hoping to get him in the balls, but with my head pushed back, I couldn't see. My aim was off and my shin slammed into his knee. Now my shin hurt too.

Axe yanked his right arm away, breaking my grip, and he hit me in the face, renewing the pain in my left eye, with the added discomfort of feeling cartilage break apart in my nose. I could feel a warm rush as blood surged from my nostril.

He was drawing back to deliver another punch to my face, when I heard tires scratching to a stop, and Axe was illuminated by headlights. I couldn't see what was happening behind me. I was almost to the point of blacking out, but I could hear car doors opening. There were voices shouting, and a glorious moment later, Axe dropped me to the ground and I sucked a breath into my lungs.

My vision cleared just enough to see the shadow of Axe standing over me, his arm extended in front of him, and there seemed to be something in his hand. My mind didn't make the connection at first, but there was a fusillade of shots, Axe's shadow disappeared from my line of sight, and then there was silence.

I was aware of footsteps as the police spread out toward me, Axe and Evelyn. I sat up and saw a cop kick the gun away from Axe's hand, but Axe gave no resistance. He was lying on his back, dead. Blood was gathering in black puddles on both sides of his body from the multiple gunshot wounds in his torso.

I was vaguely aware of people gathering around, not just near me, but on the perimeter, as neighbors came out to watch. I was also aware of more vehicles approaching, adding their headlights and emergency strobes to the illumination.

I stood up, leaning against the back of my car, as I felt a hand on my back.

"Take it easy," a police officer said, but I ignored him, looking in Evelyn's direction. Crisscrossing headlights illuminated the front of the house. There was a cop kneeling beside Evelyn, and EMTs rushed toward her with a gurney. Evelyn's face was bloodied. She wasn't moving, but she was breathing.

Another EMT came toward me and spent a few minutes examining my face and throat, shining a light in my eyes, asking how may fingers he was holding up, listening to my breathing, and countless other things I didn't feel like doing, but did anyway. He packed and bandaged my nose, and when he finished with me, I turned and saw Evelyn's gurney being loaded into the ambulance.

"Where are they taking her?" I asked my EMT.

"Boulder General," he replied as he packed up his kit.

There was still a cop standing near me, and he put up his hand.

"You can go in a bit," he said. "I need to ask you a few questions, if you feel up to it." I nodded and turned to watch as the ambulance pulled away, blue and red strobes flashing. As a few of the other vehicles had also left, it was darker now.

"I'm Officer Briggs. Your name?" I turned back and looked at Briggs, still a little flustered.

"August – " Stupid! "Arden. Arden Chase."

"This is your home?" I just nodded. He asked for my exact address and phone number, which I gave him.

"Did you know Timmy?"

"Timmy?" I echoed.

"Timmy Moskowitz," and Briggs motioned toward the body which was now being placed in a body bag by people in coveralls from the Medical Examiner's office. "Your assailant."

"His name was Timmy?" I looked down at him as they zipped up the bag and his face disappeared from view.

"Yes. Timmy Moskowitz had a long string of priors, including a few assaults with a deadly weapon."

"Huh. I was pretty sure Axe wasn't the name his parents gave him. I really wasn't expecting something like Timmy, though."

"So you *did* know him," Briggs persisted.

This wasn't getting any easier.

"No, I didn't." Briggs looked at me for a moment as if he didn't believe me. "We were never formally introduced," I capitulated.

"Did he say anything to indicate his motive for the attack?"

Shit.

"He was jealous," I sighed. "His girlfriend and I had been flirting with each other on Facebook. Axe found out."

"Had you and she had any physical contact?"

"No. We were face to face a couple of days ago, but there was no contact."

"Where was this?"

"At the Greased Hawg, on West Colfax in Denver." Briggs gave me that look again. "I know, I don't look like their typical clientele."

"Did Timmy know about this?"

"Yeah, he was there. He punched me in the face then too."

The ME people lifted the body bag onto a gurney and wheeled it toward their van.

"Was your wife aware of your relationship with Timmy's girlfriend?"

"It wasn't a relationship!" I snapped at him. "Teri and I flirted back and forth a couple of times in an online chat. That's all."

"Alright, Mr. Chase," Briggs said in a pacifying tone. "That'll be all for now." He slipped his pen in his shirt pocket and closed his notebook. "But if I could add a suggestion of my own, off the record, you might want to be careful about whose girlfriends you go palling around with."

Did he really just say "palling around"?

"Yes, sir," I said. He gave a curt nod and went toward his car, as the ME van pulled away. Briggs' car was the last one there. After he backed out and drove away, the only exterior light came from my headlights pointed toward the house, and from a streetlight half a block away, shining through the bare aspens lining my driveway.

Plodding up to the porch, I couldn't help dragging my feet. It felt like my shoes were made of lead. And as long as I'm complaining, my face hurt, my nose was throbbing and my neck felt like a tourniquet was around it, loosened just enough to allow a *little* blood up to my stupid head.

And my shirt was stuck to my chest from the gusher that had erupted from my nose a little while ago.

Could be worse, I guess. I could be in a body bag. Like Timmy.

I went in the front door and dragged myself up the stairs just long enough to change my shirt. I was downstairs again in a couple of minutes, and I turned off the living room lights, then I went back outside, pulling the door closed behind me. The door jamb was broken apart on the inside, but the latch sort of caught. At least the house didn't *look* like it was open.

I got in my car and sighed, putting my head back against the head rest. I sure could use a drink! And a nap.

I sat up and turned the key.

Lanelle sat in a chair on the back patio. She had been sobbing earlier but I was happy to see that she had stopped. As I watched, though, I could see that she was still kind of snuffling. I sat down in the chair next to hers and she looked up at me, her eyes red and puffy.

When she saw me, her face crinkled up as she started crying again, breaking my heart once more. She got up and came to me, sitting in my lap. She was fourteen years old. She hadn't sat in my lap in years. But I held her tightly as she cried, rocking slightly back and forth.

Heidi had been taken away the day of 'the incident,' and held at the animal shelter. A couple of months passed until the court made its ruling. Based on the testimony of the mail carrier, and on the gruesome photographs of his arms, as well as on the testimony of others who had witnessed Heidi's aggression over the past year, the court ordered that Heidi was to be put down.

The sentence was carried out a couple of hours ago.

Several of Lanelle's friends had been questioned about what they knew of the dog. Tony Warwick was one of them, but knowing how much Heidi meant to Lanelle, Tony said nothing about her aggression, despite the fearful encounter he himself had with Heidi on their first meeting. That elevated him a little in Lanelle's eyes, and mine.

As Lanelle's sobbing calmed again, I heard a sound behind me, and Evelyn came out on the patio.

"Oh for heaven's sake!" she said under her breath when she saw Lanelle crying on my lap. Lanelle sat up and wiped her eyes as Evelyn sat down. Lanelle leaned over and kissed me on the cheek, then got up and went inside.

I looked at Evelyn and our eyes locked like magnets. And not in a good way.

"Why can't you just let her mourn?" I asked. "She lost her beloved pet."

Evelyn sighed and shook her head.

"It was just a goddamn animal. And that animal was a pain in the ass."

"Lanelle loved her!"

"Have you ever been pepper sprayed?" she asked sharply. "No, I didn't think so. So don't try to make me feel sorry for that dog!"

"I don't give a shit if you feel sorry for the dog or not. But you could have a little empathy for your daughter!"

Evelyn blew out a disgusted sigh, shaking her head, but she didn't say anything for a while.

She had, fortunately, not given testimony in court against Heidi, but that was only because I very forcefully warned her that she would lose Lanelle if she did. I paid for that warning later, but I didn't care.

"We are NOT getting another dog," Evelyn finally said, picking up on an earlier conversation. She looked at me and raised an eyebrow in a look that was meant to put me in my place.

I just shook my head and sighed, amazed at her apparent lack of feeling.

"Dogs live shorter lives than humans, even without something like this happening," she continued emphatically. "Lanelle *will be going away to college in four years. If she gets another dog, we'll just be stuck taking care of it."*

Still, I didn't say anything.

"Lanelle said she doesn't want another dog," Evelyn argued.

"Because it's too soon!" I replied. "Heidi's loss is too fresh."

"She said she NEVER wanted to get another dog."

"She's emotional. Besides, she didn't want to fight with the fucking Ice Queen. God, I keep expecting to hear the Almira Gulch theme from the Wizard of Oz."

I looked at Evelyn and saw her lips press tightly together.

Okay, maybe I had gone a little too far.

Evelyn was unrecognizable. Her head was wrapped in bandages, including her left eye where Axe had hit her. He seemed to have had a particular fondness for that part of the face, having hit me there twice as well. There was some purplish discoloration across Evelyn's nose and cheek, where the bandages didn't cover. Her neck was immobilized with a brace, and her one visible eye was closed. She had been asleep for hours, mainly from the pain killer drip.

I fought the urge to pull the needle from her arm and jab it into my own for a few minutes.

I was sitting in an uncomfortable vinyl-covered chair which I'm pretty sure was designed by the people who brought us the rack and the thumbscrew. It was positioned in front of the window. I could tell the sun was shining, but the blinds were closed, keeping the light pretty dim in the hospital room.

The doctor had explained Evelyn's situation a few hours ago. Fortunately her injuries were not terribly serious, certainly not as serious as they looked as she lay wrapped in bandages in the hospital bed. She had a concussion, and the obvious bruising around her eye and cheek. She also had a hairline fracture on the back of her skull, where it had struck the flagstone.

But the doctor was optimistic that she could go home in the next day or so.

I looked at the clock on the wall and saw that it was 8:30. I had to think for a moment. Wednesday morning. I stood up and stretched my limbs, and I left the room and went to a little waiting room down the hall. I pulled out my phone and called Ed to let him know I wouldn't be at work today. I made a point of letting him know in detail what had happened, so that he would know I had no choice, that I wasn't just blowing off a day of work. He sounded like he understood.

I sat down in one of the chairs. Considerably more comfortable than the one in Evelyn's room. Softer, anyway.

Then I called John Parsons, Evelyn's father. That call was a little more difficult. I always had the feeling her parents didn't care that much for me. I didn't tell him why Axe had come around, just that we had been attacked. Plenty of time for the details later.

I sat back in the chair and saw the Facebook notification icon at the top. I opened Facebook and checked the notifications. This was my real profile, as Arden, and there were no notifications of any real importance. I logged out and logged back in as Augustine. There were notifications there too, including a personal message from Barbie.

"Hey, lover. I'm rubbing my nipple raw for you. Where are you?" She wasn't online now, and I had no interest in chatting with her anyway.

I was curious about Teri, though. I was sure by now that she knew about Axe. I didn't see any notifications from her.

And still nothing from JuleighAnn.

I stood and went back to Evelyn's room, sitting back down in the torture device. Despite the discomfort, I dozed off for a while.

I woke up about an hour later, feeling stiff and sore. I rotated my head, stretching my neck, trying to become a little more comfortable.

When I looked back up, Evelyn was looking at me. Even though she was awake, she was lying perfectly still, as if she was afraid to move.

"What happened?" she asked without moving her jaw. I took her hand in a reassuring gesture.

"We got beat up," I replied. "Do you remember the biker?"

She looked around at several points in the room, as if she were trying to locate the memory. She looked back at me, and I could tell by her faster breathing that she remembered.

"Where is he?" she asked quietly.

"He's dead. The police shot him."

She closed her eye, and her breathing steadied a bit. After a few moments, she opened her eye again and looked at me.

"Why?" she asked.

I guess it had to come out sometime. I held her gaze for a moment.

"Because I flirted with his girlfriend."

"He beat me up because you flirted with his girlfriend?"

"Well, I imagine you just got in his way. He was after me."

"All of this was because you flirted with his girlfriend? He got killed because you just flirted?"

"That's right."

She never looked away, boring a hole through me with her one eye.

"Why would he be that angry over a flirtation?"

"The police said he had a lot of prior convictions for several crimes including assault."

"Are you sure it wasn't more than flirting?" Amazing that, even in this position, she could still muster up *that* tone!

"Yes, Evelyn, I'm sure. As sure as I am that Tom Bratter is *more* than just a flirtation."

She pulled her hand out of mine.

"What do you know about Tom Bratter?" she asked suspiciously.

"Aside from all the publicity a year ago, not much, except that he's generous with gifts, and that you're constantly running through his mind."

"You went through my purse?" The portion of her face that I could see now displayed anger.

"No, I didn't go through your purse," I insisted, getting agitated myself. "You didn't exactly hide it very well. It spilled out onto the hall table."

Evelyn looked away now, for the first time.

"So," I continued, "how is it you felt you could get all hot with righteous indignation about me flirting with someone when you're actually cheating on me? An affair that would be an embarrassment to your father at the very least! Imagine the ethical questions that might be raised about your father's defense of Tom Bratter."

"You don't know anything about it."

"I know you don't buy a jewelry store bracelet for a casual flirtation. Not people in *our* circles, anyway."

"Well, what the hell do you expect?" she spat at me. "*We* don't have a marriage!"

"And that's news to me?" I scoffed. "Separate bedrooms, no sex for a year or more! Yeah, Evelyn, I was kind of already aware of that."

What I *wasn't* aware of was that her parents were standing in the doorway. They hadn't wasted any time coming up from Denver. Evelyn's face registered their presence, and I turned to see them. I don't know how much they heard, but her mother looked shocked. Her father was glaring at me.

"I think you'd better get out of here," he said coldly.

Like I said earlier, they weren't very fond of me.

I looked at Evelyn, who kept her eye turned away from me, and her hand clenched on her chest, out of my reach. As if I *wanted* to hold her hand. I got up and took my jacket from the back of the chair, and I walked toward them.

"I know you've never liked me much," I said as I came to a stop in front of John Parsons, "but since this may be the last time I'll have to see you, I thought I'd let you know that I never cared much for you either."

"You were never good enough for my daughter," he replied with a disdainful sneer.

"Hmm. And yet, of the two of us, *she's* the one who was actually unfaithful. With Tom Bratter."

"She didn't say that."

163

"She didn't deny it." I looked at Evelyn, then back at Parsons. "I don't know, maybe I *wasn't* good enough for her. But as it turns out, she wasn't good enough for me either. The fact is it takes two. To make it, or to break it. And she hasn't exactly come out lily-white herself."

I squeezed past her parents who were still standing in the doorway. They scarcely bothered to move out of the way.

Sweet people.

* * *

I drove aimlessly for a few hours. I couldn't really tell you what I was thinking about. It seemed like my mind was a blank. I was numb.

It was early afternoon when I pulled up in front of my house. I sat there in the driveway looking at it. At some point, Axe's motorcycle had been taken away. The house really didn't look any different than any other time.

But it looked different to me.

Don't get me wrong. It was a nice house. I knew that. But it was more house than I had ever wanted. And it was difficult to see the house without thinking of Evelyn.

And I didn't want to think about Evelyn.

I pushed the button on the remote and the garage door opened. I pulled my car in and closed the door. Pulling myself out of the car, I went inside, and I just looked around in a daze. Less than forty-eight hours ago, I was upstairs in my den having a nice, long chat with JuleighAnn. Everything was, well, not fine, but in that moment, I was completely at peace.

Now, my face had been forcibly remodeled for the second time, Evelyn was in the hospital, a man was dead, and

164

I was ultimately responsible for all of it. As if that wasn't enough, my marriage, such as it was, was over. That part in itself was no surprise. The marriage had been dead for a long time. It just hadn't fallen over yet.

And besides that, I had alienated the love of my life in the process.

Yeah, I know. Imagine *my* surprise, not only to use a phrase like 'love of my life,' but then to realize that JuleighAnn Harper was it.

I put my keys down on the kitchen counter, and I jumped when I heard the doorbell. I walked to the front entry, nervous about who might be waiting there. As I kicked the splintered pieces of the door jamb out of the way, I remembered that the front door offered little protection. I looked warily through the peephole.

My apprehension vanished when I saw Cyndi Shelton.

I tugged the door open and attempted a smile. I don't think I pulled it off, though. Cyndi's smile vanished and turned to an expression of horror.

"Oh my God!" she said. "Arden, your face looks awful!"

"Well, that's great for my self-esteem." She smiled in spite of herself, and I noticed she was holding a casserole dish. "Come on in."

Her eyes were glued to the mess on the front of my head, but she came into the entry. I closed the door behind her, then directed her into the kitchen.

"I was catering a birthday party in Greeley last night," she said, "but I heard what happened. That must have been so scary! Does your face hurt?"

"Yeah, but you should see the other guy." My memory was revisited by an image of the other guy, Timmy "Axe"

Moskowitz, lying in his own blood on my lawn, and I was immediately sorry for making the joke. Cyndi didn't seem to notice, though.

"Well, I figured you and Evelyn won't be feeling up to making dinner," she said as she put the casserole dish on the kitchen counter, "so I made you some Fettuccini Alfredo with broccoli."

"Oh Cyndi, that sounds delicious. Thank you."

"You're welcome. And here's some garlic bread to go with it," and she placed a foil-wrapped package next to it. I shook my head and tried to hide the tears welling up there. What the hell was wrong with me?

"You're such a good person." I think I managed to hide the surprise from my voice. I mean I always knew Cyndi was nice, but somehow I had managed to only see her exterior, the way she looked in my sex-starved fantasies. The sweet and sexy girl next door. I had seldom bothered to look any deeper, something I had only recently begun in my chats with JuleighAnn. I realized that my time with JuleighAnn had made me examine myself more than I had in a long time. And I didn't like what I saw.

Turns out I was unsuccessful at hiding the tears, though. Cyndi saw them and was moved to reach out and touch my arm.

"Oh, Arden," she said, her voice dripping with warmth and emotion. Just a week earlier, that along with her touch would have been enough to start the fantasies rolling. I also probably would have misread her sympathy as lust.

Now, I just wiped my eyes and shook my head again. Cyndi guided me to the kitchen table and sat me down in one of the chairs. She sat down across from me.

166

"Is Evelyn here?" she asked.

"No, she's still in the hospital." I didn't mean for it to sound as cold and uncaring as it did, but again, Cyndi didn't seem to notice.

"I'm sorry, Arden. Is she going to be okay?"

I looked at Cyndi and shook my head, which she misunderstood, because the sympathy in her eyes increased tenfold.

"No, I'm sorry," I quickly said, "she's going to be fine. I'm just amazed at your forgiving nature. Evelyn's treated you like shit, and you're still concerned about her."

"People react to pain," she said simply. "I figure when somebody treats me badly, they have pain of their own that they're dealing with."

I thought for a moment. I realized that I had been so wrapped up in my own sucky life with Evelyn that I never thought that she might be in pain as well. The two of us were such a bad match that, of course, she was unhappy too.

She was still a major pain in the ass, but at least I could understand it a little better.

"Is there anything you need?" Cyndi asked. "Anything I can do?"

If she only knew the thoughts that those questions would have ignited in my head just a few days ago!

"No, Cyndi. But thank you." I motioned toward the food she brought. "And thank you for that, too."

She nodded as we stood up from our chairs, and she put a hand on my arm again and squeezed.

"Take care," she said with a compassionate smile.

* * *

After Cyndi left, I put the Fettuccini Alfredo and garlic bread in the refrigerator. I pulled myself up the stairs and went in my den, collapsing in my chair. I started up my computer and logged into Facebook as Augustine. There were numerous notifications, including a status update from Teri.

"Axe is dead," she posted. "Shot by the police." Just the facts. Curiously devoid of emotion, but I realized that I didn't really know anything about her, or about their relationship.

There were several expressions of condolences from her friends, and I pondered whether I should add one from Augustine. I decided against it.

There was still no response from JuleighAnn, but there was another message from Barbie.

"Hey, Gus. Are you okay? Haven't seen you. I'm rubbing BOTH nipples for you baby, hoping it will bring you back."

God, is that all she ever thought about? Then I remembered my own reason for starting this profile only a week ago. How could so much have changed in such a short time?

I decided to respond.

"Hi Barbie. Sorry I haven't been around. I've been busy."

"Busy with your asshole boss, Ed?" she responded right away. I hadn't even noticed that she was currently online.

"No, just some shit I have to deal with. Nothing I can talk about. But I don't think I'll be around much." I seemed to have lost interest in what had led me to create Augustine.

"Oh, I'm sorry, Gus. Anything I can do? I'd like to make you feel better, honey."

"No, it's just stuff that I have to take care of. Thanks, though."

As soon as I sent the message, I logged out. Then I logged into my real profile, hopefully. I quickly scanned through the notifications, but there was no friend acceptance from JuleighAnn. I didn't care about any of the others. I just closed Facebook and shut down the computer.

I spent pretty much the rest of the day sitting there alone.

Yes, I was pouting. So sue me.

Dad," Lanelle said shyly as she entered my office. "Can I talk to you about something?"

"Sure, honey."

She came into my office and closed the door. She was getting tall. At sixteen years old, she was taller than her mother. She was starting to fill out now, too. She wasn't just an awkward, lanky little girl anymore. She was beginning to look like a very pretty young woman.

I had an armchair in the corner. Lanelle walked toward it rather slowly, hesitantly. She sat down and slowly looked up at me.

I was getting nervous.

"You said I could always talk to you about anything, right?" she finally asked.

"Of course," I said, passing nervous and rushing headlong into fear. Another silence ensued, which seemed to me like an eternity, though it was probably only four or five seconds.

"Well," she finally sighed, "Tony wants to take me to the Homecoming Dance."

"Oh, well that's great, honey," I said, feeling relieved. "I kind of thought he would."

"I know, but he wants to take me out afterwards, too. A bunch of friends are having an all-night party near Boulder Reservoir."

That relief I had felt suddenly careened into panic. I'd heard about that party. It was an annual thing. Had been for years. I

171

think even as far back as my senior year. More music and dancing, sometimes alcohol, often sex.

"I see," I managed. My panic continued, but Lanelle kept talking, paying no heed. Okay, so she was nervous too. Fine.

"Thing is," she said quietly, "I think I want to go, but I'm not sure."

"Why?" I said it more quietly than I intended, hoping to not reveal the shakiness of it. As a result, she didn't hear me and I had to clear my throat and repeat it.

"I think Tony wants to have sex."

I'm sure my gulp was audible.

"What about you?"

"I want to too. But I'm kind of afraid."

I waited. Barely breathing.

"I don't really know what to expect." She seemed to feel a little relieved having said that, and she leaned back in the chair.

I, on the other hand, was feeling anything BUT relieved.

"Well, honey," I said, but then I went into a long, awkward pause. "When you're sure about it, when it's someone you really care about, . . ."

"Oh my God, Dad," Lanelle interrupted, "I know how it works! That's Biology 101."

I looked at her a little confused.

"Um, well what do you want to know?"

"I asked Mom about how it feels, and what I should do."

"Yeah?"

"She said the first time will probably hurt."

"That's true."

"I think I'm ready for that. But I just didn't know how I should act during it, or what I should do. " She made a face that I wasn't quite able to interpret until she spoke again. "Mom's advice was 'fake it'."

"Fake it?" I asked.

"Yeah. She said if I want more than that, I should ask you."

I shook my head in disbelief.

"I know," Lanelle continued. "I think Mom was born without a maternal instinct." She looked at me and raised her eyebrows. "So what do you think?"

"I think I want to lock you in your room until you're thirty."

She blinked her eyes slowly, waiting for a serious answer.

I sighed.

"Well, honey, you're very young. I can't just say go for it."

"Or fake it," she interjected. I smiled.

"My advice is, be very careful."

"Yeah, I know all about safe sex."

"Yes, that is extremely important. But also, don't feel forced. Don't let Tony, or anybody else for that matter, talk you into something you don't want to do. It's your body, and you are the one with the final say. If it feels right to you, and if you're absolutely sure, it will just kind of come naturally."

I hadn't really intended for my voice to sort of fade out at the end, but that's what happened.

"Thanks," she said. She smiled a soft smile. "I know this wasn't easy."

"Oh, you noticed? You're a pretty smart kid, Lovebug."

Lanelle's smile grew.

"You haven't called me Lovebug in a while."

"You'll always be my little Lovebug."

Thursday morning was bleak. The weather was nice and sunny. I was the one who was bleak. My face hurt like you wouldn't believe, my eye once again dark blue. That color spread across my nose as well, which was still bandaged. My neck was also blue where Axe had gripped it.

I looked like shit. Felt like it too.

Evelyn had made it clear that she didn't want to see me. While I didn't say it, I was more than happy to oblige. I mean I still felt bad about the beating she took because of me, but that certainly wasn't enough to heal our relationship, even if either of us wanted it. Which we didn't, and that finality, after all this time, was adding to my gloom.

All those years of my life wasted! Okay, *our* lives.

My phone rang as I was getting ready for work. I was surprised when I saw the display.

"Lanelle!" I said. "Hi baby."

"Hi Daddy. I talked to Mom last night. I heard what happened. How are you?

"Oh, I'll live. I think it's too early to say whether that's good news or bad news."

"Dad," Lanelle said, adopting a stern tone. "How are you?"

I sighed and slipped out of my sarcastic persona.

"I'll be fine, honey. Really." I paused and thought for a moment. I decided there was no reason to put it off any longer. "I'm afraid I can't say the same for our marriage, though."

"I know. Mom kind of alluded to the same thing last night."

"Yeah? What do you think about that?"

"I think it's sad, obviously," she said. "But I know you've both been unhappy for a very long time. Frankly, I'm surprised you lasted *this* long."

"I didn't want you to be raised in a broken home."

"Well that sucks, Dad. Parents shouldn't put that on their kids. I mean I know divorce is hard on children, but so is living in a home with unhappy parents who can't stand each other."

"Wouldn't it have been harder to be shuttled back and forth between two homes?"

"I don't know. I didn't live through that scenario, so I couldn't say if it would have been harder. But I remember a lot of times, sitting there at breakfast during the cold silence. I remember seeing the anger and hatred flashing back and forth between you. I remember hearing your loudly whispered arguments. And I remember how uncomfortable all of that was for me."

"I thought we were shielding you from that."

"You know what they say about kids being perceptive. You can't really hide something that pervasive from them."

"You sure are a smart kid!"

"Yeah, I must get that from you, huh Daddy?" I smiled at that. "Anyway," she continued, "I know you're getting ready for work, so I won't keep you. I just wanted to let you know that I was thinking about you, and that I want you both to be happy."

"Thank you, honey. But I want to know how *you're* doing."

"Another time," she said. "I'm fine, but this was about you. And you have to get to work."

"I love you, baby."

"I love you too, Daddy."

Okay, so the morning just got a little brighter.

* * *

175

Despite how I felt, and how I looked, I threw myself into my job. According to Ed, he would be announcing his decision about the promotion tomorrow, and I wanted a lot of hard work to be fresh in his mind.

Just like Monday, people were curious about what happened to me, since besides an even bigger black eye, I had also added the conspicuous white nose bandage. But I gave quick responses and made my way to my office. Having missed work yesterday, there was a lot requiring my attention.

Late in the morning, as I was plowing through the stack of comps, there was a knock at my door, and Joe stuck his head in.

"God!" he said, "I heard you looked like shit today. I didn't think it could be worse than usual, but I guess I was wrong."

It looked as if he had abandoned his new asshole personality for his old, tried and true asshole self.

"Thanks, Joe. You're a real sweetheart."

"Sorry I got so pissed at you on Monday. I guess the pressure of Ed's decision about this potential promotion was getting to me."

"I know," I said, brushing it off. "Me too. It's okay."

"So how's Augustine Smith's adventure going?"

I shook my head and sighed.

"I'm kind of over it. Hasn't exactly done a whole lot for me," I replied, motioning toward my face.

"What? That's because of Augustine?" he asked incredulously.

"Ultimately. I'll tell you about it someday."

"Shit, man!" Joe always had a knack with articulation.

"Yeah. Sucks to be me, huh?"

"Yeah. Well, I see you have a lot to do, so I'll leave you alone. I just wanted to tell you I was sorry about Monday."

"Thanks, Joe. I appreciate it."

He nodded and left, closing the door behind him.

Hmm. Will wonders never cease! I don't think I'd ever known Joe to apologize for being an asshole.

I turned my attention back to the work in front of me, and I kept at it for the rest of the day, even working through lunch. And I'm happy to say that I accomplished a lot.

As I was leaving for the day, I made a point of telling Ed good night. He seemed distracted with something, but I was certain he would be impressed with everything I had gotten done.

I even impressed *myself*.

* * *

The weather had been mild for a few days, especially for December. When I went outside, though, the temperature had dipped and the sky had the look of pewter, and darkening quickly as night fell. Christmas was just a few days away, and traffic on the way home was sporadic – heavy near shopping areas, then open and fast, then slow and heavy again approaching highway interchanges.

By the time I got home, the wind had come up and snowflakes were tumbling fitfully from the sky. The house was dark, with harsh shadows cast by my headlights.

Reminded me of two nights ago, and a shiver went down my spine. I quickly pulled into the garage and closed the garage door behind me.

The leftover Fettuccini Alfredo was good and welcoming. I was eating it in front of a fire when I received a text message from Evelyn – that way, we didn't have to talk, so it was fine with me – that she was being discharged in the morning. I didn't need to do anything, though, as her parents would be bringing her home.

I dreaded coming home from work tomorrow, though.

I woke up around ten o'clock feeling disoriented. The fire had died down to embers, and the embers were almost dead by now, too. I closed the glass doors on the fireplace and picked up my plate and glass. I rinsed them out and put them in the dishwasher, knowing they couldn't be out when Evelyn got home tomorrow morning.

I climbed the stairs and, on a whim, started my computer and checked Facebook. There were a lot of notifications, since I hadn't responded to any of them in a while. Still not the one I was hoping for, though.

Not a damn thing from JuleighAnn.

Like the little girl I was apparently becoming, I felt like crying.

I shut down the computer and went to bed.

Feels like winter's on the way," I said, as I gave a final fine-tuning poke to the logs in the fire pit on our back patio. The fire was burning nicely, and I scooted my chair closer and sat down.

Evelyn didn't say anything, but she seemed happy by the fire. Or at least content in the moment.

Lanelle, sitting on the Adirondack love seat, leaned forward. She stared into the flames as if hypnotized by them, her gaze broken only when Evelyn stood up.

"I'm going to get some more wine," she said. "Either of you want anything?"

We both shook our heads and muttered thanks, as Evelyn took her glass and went inside. As she opened the door, we heard the front doorbell.

"I'll get that," Evelyn said.

Lanelle looked over at me.

"Dad," she said quietly, "about our talk a couple of weeks ago, I just wanted to let you know that I didn't."

That talk had been on my mind. The Homecoming dance and the party at Boulder Reservoir had taken place the week before, and I hadn't pressed Lanelle for details on what had happened.

But I smiled now, and Lanelle looked back into the fire.

"Tony wanted to," she continued, "but he asked me. I told him I didn't think I was ready yet. And he was fine with that."

She smiled as she looked up at me. "He said pretty much the same thing you did, that it's my body and my decision."

"Smart kid!" I said.

We both sat immobile, entranced by the fire, until the door opened and Evelyn came back out, followed by Tony. Lanelle's face lit up when she saw him.

I had noticed in the week since the party that Lanelle and Tony were practically inseparable, and that she looked at him as if he was the one who singlehandedly made the sun come up every morning. Since the party, I thought I knew what that look meant.

I realized now that I had been misinterpreting that look.

Tony sat down next to Lanelle on the love seat and Lanelle snuggled up under his arm. After he kissed her quickly, he turned to us, looking as if he were about to burst.

"I'm in!" he said.

"You're in?" Evelyn nearly echoed.

"Evelyn, no bathroom humor," I said, hoping to take advantage of her apparent good mood.

"What?" she asked, looking at me with a sneer. I guess I missed.

"Urine? Never mind." I turned back to Tony. He and Lanelle were smiling at my joke and waiting respectfully for my moment to pass. At least that's the way I chose to see it.

"UCLA School of Medicine accepted me!" he said.

"Tony, that's great!" I said, reaching over to shake his hand.

Tony had excelled at school and was graduating in the spring, a year early. He had already sent out numerous applications. I looked at Lanelle whose proud expression was tempered by the knowledge that Tony was going to be away for a year before she graduated. She looked at me.

"Well, I guess that seals it," I said to her. "I don't suppose there's any chance now of talking you into staying in Colorado for college. Denver Art Institute is pretty highly regarded." She shook her head.

"I'm still trying for the Art Institute of California," she smiled.

"San Bernardino's a long way from Boulder," I said in a tone of voice that I thought might have tempted her had she not had a stronger pull on her heart.

"I know," she said, "but it's close to Los Angeles." And she leaned closer to Tony who enfolded her in his arms.

Well, hell. I guess I wasn't my little girl's favorite guy anymore.

Friday morning was a mess. The snow had continued through the night and had accumulated and drifted for hours. I hadn't bothered to watch a weather report, and it took me by surprise. I knew the drive to work would be horrendous.

And I wouldn't be able to get on my way until I had done some shoveling.

I raced around the house getting ready, streamlining my usual routine to the bare minimum. In half the time, I was ready and opened the garage door. It looked as if at least a foot of snow had fallen, and it had drifted as deep as three feet in places.

This would definitely be a job for the snow blower.

I had bought it our first winter here, after practically blowing my back out shoveling that ridiculously long driveway. And I was a few years older now.

But wrestling the snow blower was no easy task either. It wasn't a very big one, and as deep as the snow was, my little monster kept jamming and I had to back it up frequently to clear it. I left for work a little over a half hour later than usual. I called work and left a message for Ed that I would be late.

I was relieved when I got out of Boulder, but then the highway slowed to a crawl. Snow on the highway had become packed down by previous drivers, and by snowplows pushing it around. But the driving conditions were pathetic.

I never understood why the highway department was so flummoxed by snow, here in the gateway to the Rocky Mountains. Ski towns that were actually up *in* the mountains, and which got a *lot* more snow than we did down here, somehow managed to keep up with it and keep their roads clear.

But down here, the snowplows, the trucks equipped to spread sand or magnesium chloride, well let's just say I usually didn't see much of them.

My drive to work, which usually took me about forty-five minutes, ended up being doubled. Add to that the half hour spent clearing my driveway, and it was almost 11:00 a.m. by the time I arrived at work. But even at that, I felt pretty good about myself when I saw how few people had made it in.

Felicia, the receptionist, looked up when I walked in.

"Oh, Arden," she said, "Mr. Leeson wanted to see you as soon as you got here." She never called him Ed.

"Thank you, Felicia," I said. I struggled out of my coat as I made my way toward my office. I hung it on the hook inside my door, then I checked the mirror on the back of the shelf unit that held my awards. My hair hadn't blown out of place too badly, and I was able to push it back in position, brushing the snow off of me. Nothing much I could do about the weird color on my face, or the bandage on my nose.

I took a deep breath and left my office, walking toward Ed's corner office.

This is it! I thought. He's going to tell me his decision. Either I got the promotion or I didn't.

I walked down the hallway, noticing that about half of the sprigs of plastic holly that Felicia had hung last week were drooping down. Some of them had been put back up, and a few of them had been reinforced with four or five layers of tape.

Instead of looking festive, it just looked kind of sad.

But at the moment, I didn't care. Outside Ed's door, I paused and took another deep breath. Then I reached up and knocked on the door.

"Come in," I heard from inside.

I opened the door and went inside. When Ed looked up from his desk and saw me, I could swear his face became stern.

There was no doubt when he spoke.

"Arden," he said, and his voice sounded icy. "Have a seat."

With a sudden feeling of anxiety gripping my chest, and that old sensation of butterflies in my stomach, I sat down in one of the chairs in front of his desk. Ed sat back and looked at me, narrowing his eyes a little, and he sighed.

"Arden, are you happy here?"

I thought for a moment, trying to figure out where this conversation could be going.

I didn't have a clue.

"Yes, sir. I mean I do feel a lack of creative output in my current position, but I'm looking forward to being able to change that as Senior Art Director."

I wanted to make sure he knew how badly I wanted that position. But his eyes bored into me, and I couldn't for the life of me determine what was going on here.

"You're still looking forward to being our new Senior Art Director?" he finally asked, apparently puzzled.

I shifted uncomfortably, and I felt an involuntary frown scrunch up my face, to the extent that it could, anyway, with the big bandage taped to it. I nodded my head a bit.

"Yes, I am," I said.

I watched Ed, but he still wasn't letting me in on the joke.

"Ed," I continued, "have I done something wrong?"

Finally, he sat forward and sucked in a quick breath. He reached for a manila envelope on his desk. I watched with great interest as he pulled some papers out of it.

"I received this last night," he said, looking gravely at the pages. Then he looked up at me. "Do you know what this is?"

"No, sir."

He handed the papers across his desk to me and I took them. They were just a couple of sheets of plain bond paper with text printed on them. Completely common and unnoteworthy.

Then I realized what was printed on them.

Barbie Wilcox: So, tell me about yourself.
Augustine Smith: I'm an art director for an ad agency.

Barbie Wilcox: Sounds interesting.

Augustine Smith: Well yeah, it sounds like it, but sounds can be deceiving. I mean it's an okay job but I don't have as much creative outlet as I would like. And it doesn't help that my boss is an ignorant asshole.

Barbie Wilcox: Oh, that's too bad. I'm afraid that's a pretty common complaint, though. How is he an asshole?

Augustine Smith: Oh, Ed's a jerk. Thinks he's incredibly funny and clever when he's really just embarrassing. And he's a fucking lousy manager.

Barbie Wilcox: I'm sorry honey.

Augustine Smith: He gave me the chance to do some creative stuff, and I did some really good work on it. Then the bastard snatched it away from me.

Barbie Wilcox: Hmm, that sucks.

Augustine Smith: I know. Sometimes I think I should try to find a new job, one that's more challenging and rewarding. But I do get a decent salary. I don't think I'm going to find another job that would pay me as well.

Barbie Wilcox: Well, good luck. I hope it gets better.

Augustine Smith: Thanks.

Barbie Wilcox: Gotta go. We'll talk later.

Augustine Smith: Okay, Barbie. This was very nice. Thank you.

Barbie Wilcox: Sure, lover. I'm rubbing my
nipple for you.

You know that figure of speech, 'My blood ran cold'?
It did.

"Who's Augustine Smith?" I asked, grasping for straws. Ed blew out a scoffing sound and placed a mocking smile on his face.

"You're really going to go that direction?" he asked incredulously.

I looked back down at the papers in my hand, my mind racing. I was trying not to gasp for breath, and I could hear the sound of my heart pounding in my ears. I was almost glad so much of my face was either discolored or bandaged, because I could feel it getting very flushed. I looked back up at him, at a loss for words.

"If you want to use a fake identity in your online chats, Arden, that's none of my concern," he said with a shake of his head and a shrug of his shoulders. "It's unethical, maybe even illegal, I don't know. But it doesn't concern me. However, you've revealed some very interesting things here." He held his hand out to me, and I sheepishly gave him back the papers. He glanced through them again. "It seems you think I'm an 'ignorant asshole,' a 'jerk,' and a 'fucking lousy manager'."

"Ed," I said, shaking my head, going into damage control mode, "I'm sorry. I was just blowing off some steam. I was upset about having MaxiMed taken away from me. I said some things I shouldn't have, but no harm was done."

"No harm was done?" he asked, raising his eyebrows questioningly.

"No sir. I didn't mention the name of the agency. I didn't say your last name. I didn't name the account or anything like that."

"No, you didn't," he said as he looked down at the transcript. Then he looked back up at me. "How do you suppose it will be for you and me working together from now on? Knowing that you think I'm such an ignorant asshole, and such a fucking lousy manager?"

This didn't seem to be going very well.

"Ed, I was angry when I wrote that. I didn't mean it."

"I was angry last night when I read it," he said nodding. "But I've cooled off now. I'm not angry any longer. I've made my decision based purely on logic and practicality." He put the papers down on his desk and folded his hands on top of them. "I suppose you know what I've decided."

"I'm not getting the promotion?"

Yeah, I really said that.

"No, Arden. You're not getting the promotion. What you're getting is a generous severance package, and that's based solely on your time here and on the contributions you've made to Argosy's reputation in the past."

Remember all that blood that was rushing into my face just a couple of minutes before? Well, at that moment, it all emptied back out so fast I could almost hear the sucking sound of a bathtub drain.

"Ed, please," I said, shaking my head.

"You're terminated, Arden, effective immediately. By now, there will be a building security officer waiting outside my door. You will have time to gather personal items from your office, then you will be escorted out to the elevator, down to the first floor, and out of the building."

I just sat there looking at him for a few moments.

"You're dismissed," he finally said.

I pushed myself up out of the chair, feeling exhausted. Really beat! I dragged myself to the door and left his office without looking back. And Ed was right. The rent-a-cop was standing there waiting for me. His face was inscrutable as I looked at him.

I pulled the door closed behind me and made my way back to my office. Somebody had even been nice enough to arrange for an empty cardboard box to be waiting for me on my desk. I went through my desk and around my office, gathering up my personal things and my Addies.

It didn't take as long as I thought it would.

I put my coat on and picked up the box. The building jarhead opened the door, and as I slowly walked out, he fell in step behind me. The few people who were there saw me leaving. Some looked at me with sympathy, others with surprise.

I continued on my walk of shame out of the office-lined hallway and into the lobby. Joe was there talking to Felicia. They both looked up as I came into view.

Joe turned toward me and had an enigmatic look on his face. I went toward him and started to tell him goodbye, but his expression changed to a crooked smile.

And he raised a finger to his chest and rubbed his nipple through his shirt.

* * *

On my drive back home, I tried not to think about Barbie. About the sex chats we had engaged in. About the fact that she was really Joe.

I hated Joe right then. And Ed.

But mostly, I hated myself. Talk about an ignorant asshole! If there was an Assie award, I could add it to the awards in my box.

The main reason, though, that I was trying not to think about that was that I needed my wits about me for driving. It was still cold, but the sun had come out. That meant that a lot of the snow had turned to icy slush, resulting in slick driving conditions and lots of dirty splashback from the cars around me.

And there were a lot of cars. The noon hour on a Friday just before Christmas was not a good time to be driving in hazardous conditions while plotting revenge.

Who was I kidding, though? There was no revenge to be had. I had played the game, made some really stupid choices, and lost.

And now I was out of a job.

What the hell was I going to do now? Forty-nine years old and I just got fired. But I decided it would have to wait. I'd think about it later. For now, I just needed to get home. I felt like shit and I needed a little peace and quiet.

What I got was Evelyn and her parents. God, what a day!

Evelyn, her head still bandaged, but the neck brace gone, was lying on the sofa in the family room, in front of the fireplace. Her mother was sitting in a chair near her, and her father was stoking the fire.

They all looked at me curiously when I came in. And they saw the box in my hands. I didn't say a word. I just plodded up the stairs and into my den.

I had just sat down at my desk when there was a knock on my door.

"Shit!" I said under my breath. I closed my eyes and sighed, hoping, I think, that I had just imagined it. When the knock sounded again, I opened my eyes.

"Yes?"

The door opened and John Parsons came in. Even though he had been retired for a year, he still dressed in a suit and tie, looking every bit the lawyer he used to be.

"Do you mind?" he asked. I silently shook my head, too drained to speak if it wasn't absolutely necessary. He closed the door behind him. I motioned toward the armchair I had in the corner, and he sat down there. He glanced at the box that I had brought home, then he looked back at me.

"Arden, Evelyn has told us that she wants a divorce."

"Really?" I replied. "I guess you forget that *I* was the one who introduced the idea yesterday in the hospital room."

Apparently I wasn't too exhausted to be a smartass.

I looked at him with a face that would have been devoid of expression even if it *wasn't* for the big bandage and the hefty hematoma. Parsons didn't seem fazed by it, though. He kept looking at me with his piercing lawyer eyes.

"At any rate," he continued with an irritated sigh, "she wants it to be quick and easy. She's not asking for maintenance. She wants the house and her car, as well as some of the furniture, to be divided among you."

He glanced at the box again, and thought for a moment.

"Considering what you have put into this house," he continued, "rather than ask you to just sign it over to Evelyn, and considering the situation you apparently now find yourself in," and he glanced pointedly at the box again,

"I'm prepared to offer you twenty-five thousand dollars to walk away from here and not bother her again. That should help you to get back on your feet, and will hopefully provide enough incentive for you to leave Evelyn alone and not talk to anyone about her and Tom Bratter."

Okay, I admit I wasn't expecting that. I was aware that the whole Tom Bratter thing was a pretty potent topic, but I never considered the possibility that it could turn out to be a source of income for me.

My reaction was more physical than verbal. I exhaled in surprise almost as if I had been punched in the stomach, but in retrospect, I realize that it probably sounded like a scoffing sound. Parsons apparently misread it too, and he looked a little nervous.

"Alright," he continued, "fifty thousand. Take it or leave it."

I wondered if that really was his final offer, or if I could get more out of him. But I didn't want to risk it.

"Okay," I said, trying to keep my voice steady. "I'll take it."

With a steely smile, he reached in his coat pocket and pulled out his check book.

I certainly wasn't going to tell him that I would have paid *them* to take her away and make her leave *me* alone.

Well, I would have if I still had a job.

* * *

I spent the rest of the afternoon sitting in front of my computer, examining my situation. It wasn't as bad as I might have thought when I first learned that I lost my job. I had my severance package and a very nice 401K from work. I had a few thousand stashed away in a savings account that I could dip into without penalty if I needed to.

And there was the check from John Parsons.

I figured I could live for at least a couple of years on my available funds.

Not that I wanted to use up my savings. I needed to get another job. But realistically, I knew that could take a while. I was a middle-aged man who had gotten fired from his last job, and I didn't really expect a glowing recommendation from Ed.

I also knew I couldn't go job hunting just yet, looking the way I did.

It really didn't take me all afternoon to ponder what I just said in a couple of paragraphs. The time was also peppered with lots of soul-searching and self-inflicted ass kicking. I knew that if I hadn't been such a horny muttonhead last week, I'd still have a job, and in fact, maybe even a better one as of today.

But I had to give in to my gonads and embark on my genitalia junket. And look what it had gotten me.

To the mental list I had started compiling the other night, of all the problematic things I had accomplished in such a short time, I could now add that I had lost my job and my home.

Way to go, Arden.

I was starting my second J&B of the evening, having successfully avoided the Parsons party downstairs, when I heard a ping from my computer. I had left Facebook on in the background, and I had received a personal message.

I didn't really expect to hear from "Barbie" again, but I thought it was possible that Teri might try to get in touch.

As I pulled it up, though, I realized it was my own profile, as Arden Chase, that was still open.

And the message was from JuleighAnn. She had accepted my friend request and was making contact. I hesitated, almost dreading what she had to say.

Then I told myself that I was being a moron. She had accepted my friend request, so how bad could it be?

Haven't you been paying attention to the last few days? I responded to myself.

Well, enough of that. I opened the message window.

"Hello, Arden," she said. "I find myself wanting to call you Gus, but I realized that I like the name Arden better.

"I've spent the last few days thinking about what you told me. I admit that I was hurt at first, finding out that you weren't who you told me you were. I had been hurt and lied to in the past, and this dredged up those old feelings. I liked you very much, as Augustine, and was surprised to find how strong my feelings had grown for you in such a short time. So that added to the hurt.

"But after thinking about it for a couple of days, I realized how difficult it must have been for you to tell me the truth. I know that took a lot of courage. And I was so happy when I saw how much you liked me as well.

"So after some self-examination, I've reached the conclusion that if I liked you as Augustine, I'll probably like you as Arden."

Baby alert: I had tears in my eyes as I read that. But you know what? I don't even care what you think of me anymore. JuleighAnn Harper, the most wonderful and beautiful woman on Facebook, really liked me.

The *real* me. Arden Chase.

While I knew she was online, I quickly responded.

"JuleighAnn, I'm so happy to see your message. And again, I am incredibly sorry for my earlier deception."

"It's okay," she replied. "I understand. I don't know all the details of your life, but based on what you said, and on the steps you took to get away from it for a while, I can only guess that it must be pretty bad."

"Well, in a way, it's getting better. I mean there's been some major shit in the fan action during the last few days, and some of that shit will still be on me for a while. But despite the smell, things are starting to look up."

I waited a bit, and it took her almost a minute to respond. But she finally did.

"So, you're married, huh?"

"For now," I replied. I thought about how much to say, but I saw right away that she was typing a response.

"I think that's the part that hurt the most," she said. "Because I had come to like you so much, finding out that you were married and unavailable was almost like a punch in the face."

"I know a little bit about that," I said.

"You said that your marriage was the biggest contributing factor in your unhappy life."

"Yes, but I don't make any claims that it was as bad as the relationship you were in. It wasn't a physically abusive marriage. Just full of anger and resentment and indifference."

"Well," JuleighAnn replied, "indifference can be almost as hurtful as physical abuse." After another pause, she continued. "You also said that you've just about reached your limit with the marriage."

"Yes, that's actually one of the things that are looking up. The marriage is over and the divorce will be quick and easy, and handled to the satisfaction of both parties."

"We've never even met in person," she mused. "We only know each other from online chats, and that for only about a week. It's crazy that we could have fallen so hard so fast."

"I know it is, JuleighAnn. Believe me, that's been one of the biggest puzzlers on my mind over the last several days."

"I don't even know if you're any good in the sack. Maybe that's why your marriage sucks."

Have I said that I *really* liked this lady?

"You know," I said, "not to downplay the sex skills of either one of us, but I've been thinking lately that sex isn't even that big a deal. I mean it would be great, and I would love it. Don't get me wrong. But what I've been wanting so much since getting to know you is just to be able to touch you, to hold you in my arms. To press your body against mine - not in a sexual way, but in mutual affection. To feel our hearts beating close together.

"Then I think, 'What the hell is wrong with you, you moron? She's hot!'

"Sorry if I spoiled the mood. I was serious about what I said above, though."

"That sounds pretty nice," she responded. "That kind of sums up what I've been thinking too. How did this happen exactly?"

"I don't know," I replied. "You were just you, and I was – well, I was somebody else. But even then, it was still me. And we just seemed to click."

"That's a very convoluted explanation," she replied, but she followed it with a smiley.

"Well, it's been a pretty convoluted relationship so far. But I'm hoping that, since we're so close to each other, geographically, we can maybe make it a little more straightforward and uncomplicated."

"I'd like that," she said. "Maybe we can meet in person. I'd like to actually see your face while I talk to you."

Hmm.

"Uh, JuleighAnn, about my face, there's something I should tell you."

"Oh great! Now what?"

*J*ust a few months ago, on a beautiful late summer day, two days before Lanelle left for Los Angeles, she and I went for a hike in Chautauqua Park to mark the occasion. Well, maybe hike isn't the right word. We took a more leisurely walk along one of the many trails for a bit, but we didn't get near the Flatirons this time.

On the way back, we ended up on my isolated park bench. It was partially surrounded by pines and aspens, but with an unobstructed view of the Flatirons in the distance.

"How is it I never knew about this spot?" Lanelle asked.

"I have only just begun to impart the vast treasury of my knowledge to you, child," I said. She looked at me out the corner of her eye and shook her head. Then I went in for the kill. "And now you're leaving me."

"Oh," she said in a somewhat whimpery tone. She leaned toward me and slipped her arm through mine, putting her head on my shoulder. I put my arm around her and kissed the top of her head.

We sat like that for a while, watching the clouds chase each other over the Flatirons, fascinated by the shadows that slipped down the inclined planes of the rocks. Lanelle, I'm sure, thought I was just a nature lover. Fact is I was trying to keep my emotions in check.

Damn, I was going to miss this kid!

I don't know how much time passed. There was little to determine its passing other than the westward journey of the sun. And I was never good at telling time by the sun.

Lanelle sat up when I reached into a cargo pocket of my shorts with my free hand. I pulled out a small package and handed it to her. She glanced up at me, then took the package in her hands.

"What is this?" she asked.

"Just a little something to let you know how special I think you are."

"Special, huh? You couldn't spring for some real wrapping paper?" I had wrapped it in a single piece of brown paper.

"Just thinking of you, Lovebug," I smiled. "I didn't want you to have to go to too much trouble to open it."

She grinned as she pulled the paper off, revealing the gift I had made for her. It was a little commemorative book, small enough to go in a pocket or purse, containing copies of photos and art, marking different moments in her life.

I watched her face as she leafed through it, smiling at her changing expressions. They were mostly happy expressions, though her smile turned a little sad when she saw a picture of Heidi.

She seemed to want to hug me, but since her hands were occupied with turning the pages, she just leaned to the side until her shoulder was pressed against mine. I leaned against her too, staying quiet until she got to the end, a picture of me with the caption, "World's Greatest Dad!"

Lanelle closed the little book and wrapped her hands around it in a miniature hug. Then she looked up at me with tears in her eyes, and she put her arms around my neck. Her hug almost squeezed some moisture from my own eyes, as I've heard could happen in some situations. I managed to hold it back as I hugged her.

She sniffed and pulled away.

"My little girl's all grown up now," I said.

"Really, Dad? You're using that old cliché?" But she smiled as she wiped her eyes.

"Sometimes clichés work. You're going out on your own. You'll be a thousand miles away from us now."

"No, not a thousand miles," she countered with a disbelieving tone.

"Nine hundred eighty-four miles from Boulder to San Bernardino," I said. "I checked."

"God! I didn't realize it was that far." I could see that the knowledge had a negative effect on her. She was staring down at the ground a few feet in front of us.

Me and my big mouth.

"But you won't be alone," I said, trying to overturn the mood I had introduced. "Tony will be there with you."

Her face instantly warmed up with a smile, the likes of which I had never seen before. This girl was in love!

She looked back up at me, still smiling. But as she looked at me, the smile faded into a somewhat wistful look.

"I hope you and Mom find some happiness," she said.

Huh! In that moment, my smartassery abandoned me. I was at a loss for words.

I put my arm around her and, finding the approximate location on the ground in front of us that she had been staring at a moment before, I commenced staring myself. Lanelle leaned against me and I kissed the top of her head again.

"I love you, Daddy," she said.

"I love you too, little one."

I moved out on Saturday morning. I was pleasantly surprised at how quickly I was able to organize it, but you can find and arrange anything online nowadays. I didn't take much – the contents of my den and my bedroom, a couple of chairs and a coffee table from the living room, and the little kitchen table and chairs.

Finding movers on such short notice was a little harder, but I located a day labor place that provided a couple of young men for a couple of hours. That was long enough to load my meager possessions into the small rental truck, and then unload them in the apartment that I found.

I had focused my home search closer to where I thought the greater concentration of jobs would likely be, so I moved away from Boulder and into Lakewood, due west of Denver.

Yeah, that's the town where JuleighAnn lived. So what?

After seeing the doctor for a follow up examination of my nose, and fortunately a downgrade of the big, scary bandage, I spent the rest of the day unpacking and settling into my little apartment. It was kind of dumpy, but it was only temporary. I signed a six month lease with the intention of finding a better place after I got a job.

On Sunday, I drove to a nice little park a few blocks south of Colfax Avenue. It was chilly, but there was a beautiful Colorado blue sky overhead, and most of the snow from a couple of days before had melted. There were several stands of bare and brittle looking aspens and cottonwoods, but these were punctuated by evergreens which provided some areas of privacy.

She was sitting alone on a bench beside one of these groupings of spruce trees. I had just walked across a footbridge and I stopped in my tracks the moment I saw her. The dog noticed me first, turning his head in my direction, but that movement caught JuleighAnn's attention and she turned.

She stood up and Molson followed suit, coming toward me as far as the leash would allow. I took a nervous breath and started forward. After he glanced backwards towards JuleighAnn, Molson apparently realized that I wasn't a threat, so he was wagging his tail expectantly, and shifting back and forth as I approached.

As I reached him first, I knelt down on the path and petted him, scratching the underside of his ears and under his collar. I've never known a dog that didn't like that. Then I stood back up and looked at JuleighAnn.

She was beautiful, her dark hair gleaming in the morning sunlight. Her breaths came out in little clouds of steam in the cold air, and I realized as I looked at her that they started coming a little faster.

Mine did too.

I walked toward her, just looking at her face, at her sparkling green eyes. And the whole time, I was wondering about the protocol for meeting an online friend/lover in real life. I had never been in this position before, and I wasn't sure what was expected. Or allowed.

In the end, I tossed the thoughts aside and went with what felt natural.

I reached up and placed my hands gently on the sides of her face, and neither one of us had broken our intense gaze. Upon making physical contact, we both held our breath, and I realized that, in keeping with my recently increasing emotionalization, there were tears in my eyes. I leaned forward, touching my lips to hers. They were soft, inviting, and she leaned into me.

At that, I wrapped my arms around her, burying my face in her hair, and we stood, almost oblivious to Molson romping about us. I don't know how long we stood like that, holding each other tightly, but when we finally came apart, JuleighAnn looked at me and smiled.

"Hi, Gus," she said.

Yeah, she was a smartass too.

The divorce was indeed quick and easy. We didn't have to spend any time in a courtroom, or even meeting with a mediator. In keeping with our agreement, John Parsons directed it all, and it was over before my six month lease was up.

I had been spending a lot of time at JuleighAnn's house. It was just as she had described it. It looked out over a pretty little lake, surrounded by cottonwoods, a very peaceful and idyllic setting.

"You know," I said one sunny afternoon in early June, "I could get used to this." We were sitting on her deck, watching the activity in her trees as birds fluttered tirelessly among the feeders. All the birds seemed to ignore Molson who was busily sniffing around the yard. Down the hill and beyond the fence, the lake glittered in the sunlight.

"Yeah?" JuleighAnn replied as she looked at me from the corner of her eyes and took a sip of her white wine sangria. "Prove it."

"Huh?"

"Your lease is almost up. Why don't you move in here? You already spend most of your time here anyway."

I looked at her with a smile. She was sprawled out on her chaise lounge, one hand behind her head, looking incredibly sexy and relaxed. She put her glass down and looked at me. I realized that she was serious.

"You're not concerned about a poor, unemployable old geezer living under your roof?"

"I've pretty much gotten used to it by now," she said with a smirk.

"You've gotten used to it?" I said with raised eyebrows. "You're not even going to bother to refute the 'old geezer' remark?"

"That's not my place, baby," she replied with a serious tone. "I don't like to argue with you. And you *are* nine years older than I am, after all."

I think I had met my match.

She was right about my spending so much time here. I had all but given up on finding a job with another ad agency or design studio. They were mainly hiring younger creatives, especially those right out of art school. Kids who were more malleable, and who didn't expect as much money.

But that situation had actually proven to be a catalyst for a better situation. I had used my advertising skills, and some contacts that I retained from my job, to arrange an exhibit of some of JuleighAnn's photography. And with a few photographs, we had even combined our talents and created some multimedia pieces with her pictures and my verse.

I'm proud to say that those ended up being some of the most popular pieces.

The week-long exhibit itself was a moderate success. It was a small venue, so attendance was fairly low to begin with, but her work was strong enough that it attracted attention. Then, a very nice article was written about her photography in the Arts section of the Denver Post, which resulted in much better attendance for the last few days, and several sales.

The *coup de grace* was when a local gallery signed her for a long term exhibition.

Which was great for JuleighAnn, but the whole episode also initiated a new beginning for me. Those contacts I had managed to retain from my job were providing some income as I had begun taking on some design and promotion work on a freelance basis. I wasn't making a lot of money, but I was paying the bills.

"I don't recall you complaining about my age last night," I continued. "I think I managed to keep up with you." JuleighAnn turned out to be an exciting and energetic lover.

"I'm not *complaining* about it now," she replied nonchalantly. "Just an observation." She looked at me through narrowed eyes. "I *did* notice you were breathing pretty hard, though."

I looked at her face and smiled. I allowed my eyes to wander downward, over the appealing bulges of her clingy tank top, and down to her long golden legs and bare feet.

"Well, it *was* way past my bed time," I said. "I mean what was it, eleven o'clock?"

"It was nine o'clock," she replied.

"Yeah, but that's eleven o'clock Boston time." I looked out over the back yard and saw that Molson had found a sunny spot between the trees and had settled down for an afternoon nap. "I think I've gotten my second wind now."

JuleighAnn drained the last swallow of her sangria. Then, smiling, she sensuously stood up and walked toward the door into the house.

"Okay, let's see whatcha got, old man."